BILLIONAIRE NEEDS NANNY

RIVER LAURENT

Billionaire Needs Nanny

978-1-911608-38-7

BLURB

I'm a nanny and I'm telling you now, some jobs are just created in hell!

Your boss is so hot, your panties combust and burn your skin. You put the fire out by avoiding his peacock green eyes and those sensuous lips. The way his tongue came out to caress that forbidden bottom lip… Oh, God. You scold yourself for those impure thoughts and promise you will not take a bite of that forbidden apple.

Then you meet his daughter and she takes an instant dislike to you. It's okay, you tell yourself. You've always liked a challenge. Anyway, you're a child whisperer, and there isn't a child in the world you cannot tame.

But then you meet the ex-wife…

Like I said, some jobs are created in hell.

ACKNOWLEDGMENTS

Thank You

Leanore Elliott
Brittany Urbaniak
Kristin Moran

Chapter One

HANNAH

I adjusted the skirt that stopped at my knees and made sure my button-down top wasn't showing too much cleavage. I knew I was fiddling with my outfit because my stomach was in knots. I pushed back my stray honey-blonde hair and tucked it behind my ear. Why did every job interview make me so unnecessarily nervous? I'd done them a good hundred times by now, but that didn't matter. Each new one was the same—a jittery mixture of excitement and fear in the pit of my stomach.

Why, I don't know.... I was good at what I did.

Hell, I started off as a babysitter when I was eleven years old, and as I grew older, I just kept on doing it because I loved kids so much. I was a natural when it came to understanding and handling them. I was like one of those horse whisperers, only I was doing it to children. There wasn't a child yet, I hadn't managed to befriend or love.

Maybe I was extra nervous with this one because my employer would be Christian West. He was one of the richest men in California, a billionaire. And he was paying well above the going rate. Working for him would mean I'd be financially stable for a few years, and I could really use all the stability I could get after taking on a mortgage on the little condo I lived in.

I locked my cozy home, walked down two flights of stairs, and out into the glorious morning sunshine. Slipping into Betsy, my trusty old Mini, I gave her a little pep talk about making it without any stops to my destination. Betsy was old, you see, and couldn't make long drives anymore. My father gave her to me when I first learned to drive. I still remember that day. Dad had tied a massive pink ribbon around her. She was a secondhand car and there were a few scratches on her even then, but I was so happy I started crying.

Christian West's house was about an-hour out of town, but I was sure she could make it. I turned the key and she spluttered to life.

"Good girl," I whispered.

It was Sunday and the streets were mostly quiet. Like the trooper she was, Betsy made it to the most impressive set of black gates I'd ever seen. Someone must have been watching for my arrival because the gates swung open, and I drove through. After parking in the circular driveway, I stepped out of my car and glanced around at the impeccable landscaping. Wow, how wonderful to live in such utterly beautiful surroundings. I mean I loved my little home, but this... Wow! It was truly something else.

I adjusted my hair in the rearview mirror quickly and once I was sure there wasn't a strand out of place, I snagged my resume, straightened my spine, and got out. Taking a deep breath of fresh morning air I began to walk up to the big double doors. It was so peaceful and quiet my heels were loud on the driveway, filling the still air with a noise that felt foreign to it.

"Okay Hannah, you can do this."

The house was huge and dramatic. White stucco walls bordered with dark green perfectly manicured greenery made the three-story high structure look sleek and modern. Everything was done with such perfect detail and precision that I knew without a doubt it would be just as immaculate on the inside. I was pretty certain the owner of this piece of real estate was high on the OCD scale.

But I could deal with OCD.

I raised my hand towards the doorbell and suddenly felt paralyzed with fear. I took a deep breath and exhaled slowly. *You can do this Hannah. You're good at this remember?* I took another deep, calming breath. *He's not an ogre. Just a man who needs help with his daughter.* I exhaled. When I felt like I had my nervousness under control, I pressed the bell and waited. Shifting my weight from one foot to the other, I tried to think positive thoughts.

The door swung open and a man appeared.

I sucked in a breath of sheer amazement. Oh, my God! He was gorgeous. Far, far more gorgeous than any photo I had seen on the net. And he was tall. Very tall. I wasn't a short person at all, but he made my five foot eight look like nothing in comparison. I knew he had to be at least six foot four, maybe even five. I wanted to say something, but I couldn't. I just never expected him to answer his own door. It completely took me by surprise. I was expecting a housekeeper, or butler, or whoever rich people hire to answer their doors. I gaped at him like a demented goldfish.

He had shimmering emerald green eyes. They burrowed into mine. "Hannah Gray?"

I shook myself awake. "Yes," I said in a weird voice. I never realized I could sound that squeaky. I swallowed the frog in my throat, and hurriedly shoved my hand out toward him. "Yes, yes, that's me, Hannah Gray. You must be Mr. West. I'm here about the nanny position," I blabbered unnecessarily, since he obviously knew who I was.

He took my hand and a shot of electricity ran up my fingers. My eyes widened as I fought the instinctive impulse to pull my hand away.

Christian West's lips pressed into a straight line, as he looked me up and down.

Suddenly, I felt self-conscious about my outfit. I shouldn't have worn this blouse. It made my breasts look even bigger than they were, and this skirt was too fitting... I should have worn something longer. Something that wouldn't have made his eyes grow frosty. I forced myself not to tug my skirt down under his disapproving gaze.

"You're early," he said coldly, as he released my hand and stepped back.

"I hope that's not a problem," I mumbled. "I was...umm... anticipating more traffic. I hope I'm not disturbing you. I can go away and come back in twenty minutes."

"It's fine. I just wasn't expecting you yet. Come inside."

Chapter Two

HANNAH

I stepped over the threshold and he closed the door behind us. The sound echoed down the hallway.

"Follow me please," he instructed distantly.

I nodded and followed him meekly enough, but hell, was I all eyes or what? He was dressed in a blue button-down shirt with the sleeves rolled up. It showed off muscled forearms. Not the kind body builders pumped up on steroids had, but the kind that woodsmen or fishermen had. Years and years of hard labor. In his case, I guess, training.

The expertly cut shirt didn't hide how stupendously built he was. The dark slacks he wore fitted him perfectly and showed off his firm full ass. Firm full ass? What the hell was I thinking? *Stop having inappropriate thoughts! This is probably going to be your boss, you nincompoop.* Biting my lip, I quickly glanced back up and forced myself to glance around as we walked down the hall.

As I expected, the whole place was professionally and tastefully decorated. It was like being inside a magazine spread. Very beautiful, but it seemed to miss that personal touch and warmth of a real home. My own place was cluttered with crap I'd brought back from vacations, photos with my family and my friends, and an assortment of random things I'd found in junk shops and fell in love with. It definitely wasn't as immaculate and beautiful as this house, but it was warm and inviting. And it was all mine... at least while I kept up the mortgage payments.

We reached his office. The door was already open. He walked in and waved to a chair across his desk. As he went around it, I settled down into the insanely plush chair. Instead of sinking into it, I was careful to keep my back straight. On his desk was the first signs of a family. A photo of a little girl. I guessed that was his daughter.

"Can I get you anything, Hannah?"

The way he said my name made shivers run up my spine. I opened my mouth to answer, and his eyes flickered up and down my body again. I watched his tongue slip out and caress his bottom lip, and I could have sworn he was attracted to me too. The thought was enough to make me force my thighs together. "No, I'm okay," I said without stumbling over my words... too much.

Mr. West nodded and pulled out a paper from a stack on his desk.

I already knew it was the resume the agency had sent on my behalf. Enclosed was also a copy of the thorough background check I'd submitted to. It was very intrusive, but it came with the territory. You could never be too careful with who you allowed around your children. They were the most precious things you had.

"I see you have a lot of experience," he said, looking over the sheet in his hands. "And your references are glowing." He pierced me with a look. "Someone actually said you were a heaven send for her twins."

I waved a hand modestly. "They were lovely kids, honestly. I never had much of an issue with them, and whenever I did, they were actually easy to calm down. I always got along with kids."

"Uh... huh... what about difficult children? Have you taken care of any?"

I nodded. "Of course. I've been taking care of kids since I was eleven years old, so it's almost impossible not to run across a problem child or two."

He leaned forward in his chair and rubbed a hand over his dark, deliciously stubbly chin. "How do you handle it?"

It was clear he had absolutely no idea how gorgeous he was when he did that. I cleared my throat. "I usually find some common ground with the child and go from there. Most of them just want to be heard, want extra attention, or have been a bit spoiled and need to have their limits laid out for them. When they see that someone understands them, then they go right back to being their amazing selves."

Christian pursed his lips as he looked back at my resume. "Hmm..."

I was caught between the uncomfortable feeling of wanting to climb over the desk and sit in his lap and the acute sensation he would rather not hire me even though he knew I would be great for the job.

I wished I could just come out and ask what the problem was, but I didn't want to make it weird.

He finally put the document down on his desk and glanced up at me. Once more, his eyes took me in like he was taking a mental picture of every inch of me.

He was making it so hard for me to focus.

"I would sometimes require you to work all week. I work till late at night and I need someone reliable for Annie in the evenings. Would that be a problem?"

"I don't mind putting in the extra hours."

“I might need you on some Saturdays as well."

"I can do that," I chimed in quickly.

“I live in the city for most of the week and only come back here on the weekends, which means you will be working most of the time at my place in the city. Are you all right with that arrangement?"

“No problem.”

I could tell he still wasn't completely sold on the idea of me as his daughter’s nanny, but I knew he was wrong. I would be great. Especially, if she was as difficult as he was trying not to show she was. It would be a challenge I would enjoy. Besides, the job had great pay and benefits. Not to mention the boss was so hot I could stare at him all day. What more could anyone ask for?

Stop that!

"Is there anything else I should know about the position?" I asked politely, so things wouldn't stall out.

"My daughter means the world to me," he said slowly. He leaned back in his seat and seemed to grow a bit tenser. "Annie's had a... well... hard time lately, so she can be difficult sometimes. I want to make sure that won't be an issue for you."

I shook my head. "Not at all. As I said before, I've worked with every range of child. From troubled to special needs. I don't have a problem with any of it. I have a lot of patience and some techniques to help keep them calm, distracted, or whatever it is that they need."

"You seem very sure of yourself," he commented, as that big beautiful hand came up and rubbed at his square jaw again.

I sat up a little taller. "I take pride in what I do. Taking care of kids gives me purpose and makes me happy. I'm good at it, Mr. West. I promise you won't be disappointed if you hire me."

His eyes seemed to pry into my very soul as he picked up the sheet with all of my info on it and tucked it into a folder.

My heart sank. I knew he wasn't sold on me. I clutched my purse a little harder. I could feel my cheeks burning with embarrassment. I had practically pleaded for this job.

Then he looked up at me with those incredible green eyes. They were clear. He had made a decision. "Call me Christian, and when can you start?"

I stared at him in surprise. Was he really asking me to work for him? His expression was so guarded and cold. I still couldn't tell what he really thought about me, but hey, at least he was giving me a chance.

I smiled at him. An unguarded, ecstatic smile.

Then for a fraction of a second, he seemed to soften. Then that shroud of mystery fell right back into place. He put the file away in a drawer.

I watched him lock it, then look at me with an expectant expression, before I realized I still hadn't answered him. "Oh! I can start tomorrow. I have a clear schedule."

"Good," he replied, as he pushed back and stood up. ""You can turn up at my apartment in the city. The address is on the last page of your contract, but before we finalize anything, or sign any paperwork you should meet Annie."

I stood up and shouldered my purse. "I'd love to."

“Have you had the chickenpox?”

I smiled. “Yes, I had it as a child. Life-long immunity.”

“Good. Annie is recovering from an infection.”

“Poor kid.”

“Indeed.”

We walked through the vast house without speaking, our shoes echoing in the silent hallways.

Through an open door, I could see the kitchen was huge and spotless. When I glanced through large ceiling to floor windows, I spotted a huge pool in the backyard. It felt as if the house was expanding. The more we walked the more there was to see.

It felt uncomfortable to me to be walking together without conversation, but it clearly suited him. I shot him a sidelong glance. I was so intensely aware of him, my skin throbbed. I had never felt this way about any man before.

We climbed a grand marble staircase and walked down a corridor.

Christian knocked on a door lightly before he opened it...

I melted at the sight of the little girl. One day, she would be a heartbreaker, but at the moment she was just the cutest, most beautiful angel I ever saw. Actually, she looked a lot like him. Her raven hair pulled into a ponytail and her green eyes were big and round. She was utterly, completely and totally adorable and she knew it.

His eyes had softened and he smiled as he looked at her. So much love and adoration poured from the stern man that I could feel it in the air. He crossed the room.

I held back and watched the situation unfold.

The little girl glanced up at us and then back down at the phone in her hand.

"Annie, I want you to meet your new nanny, Miss Gray."

Annie, her little face still full of red spots, glanced up at me again, pressed her lips together tightly, flipped onto her stomach, and languidly kicked her legs in the air. Her shoulders drew up closer to her ears as she peered down at her phone's screen as if it was the only important thing in the room.

This wasn't going to be easy.

But that was okay.

I liked a challenge.

"You don't want to say hi?" Christian asked as he moved closer and sat on the bed beside her.

Annie shook her head.

Her father rubbed her back lightly.

She ducked her head under her father's arms and secretly cut a hateful glare my way.

Okay, I wasn't expecting that.

She clearly didn't want me here, but I didn't have even a moment of uncertainty. If the little madam thought I'd give up just like that, she had another think coming. I would get this child to be my friend if it killed me.

Chapter Three

HANNAH

"Alright, I've got some paperwork to sort out with Miss Gray. Maybe we could watch a movie together, after that."

Annie perked right up. "Really?"

"Really?"

"Do I get to pick?"

"Maybe."

"I know what. I'll pick a selection and you can pick from that."

"Fine," he conceded,

"Yes!" she shouted as she hopped off the bed and bounced over to the TV. She picked up the remote and started going through movies.

Christian laughed, a deep smooth sound. "But just give me a little while, okay? Play your game, and I'll be back."

Something about a single dad and a child had always been my weakness. That gorgeous hard edge only softened by love was enough to make me melt. I wanted to see that smile on Christian's lips again. It just came off as so sweet and comforting.

"I'll bring some snacks up for us," he said, standing and pushing his hands into his pockets. "Anything you want in particular?"

"Popcorn and juice," she said distractedly as she found a movie that drew her eye.

"Juice and popcorn, it is."

"Okay, Daddy."

As soon as we left the room, the smile was gone from Christian's face again. That same distant coldness filled the space between us as we walked downstairs together.

I cleared my throat and tried to clear away the awkwardness I felt. "She seems sweet."

"She is," he agreed as we stepped off downstairs. "She has a hard time letting new people in, but she's not a bad kid."

"I'm sure she isn't," I said politely. “Uh... where is the rest of the staff?”

He cut his eyes in my direction. "They are attending a wedding. One of the maids is getting married.”

We walked in silence until we ended up back in his office where he rooted around in a drawer and produced a set of keys.

I took them and clutched them in my palm. He stood so

close to me I swear I could feel his body heat if I leaned in just a little.

"You can start tomorrow morning. Arrive at about seven. Be on time. Take the paperwork with you and bring it back tomorrow signed." He pointed at the file in front of me. "Mrs. Bennet, my housekeeper has included a file on Annie's diet and schedule in there."

"Sure, great. Uh... Mr. West, I mean Christian. Thank you for giving me the job. I promise you won't regret it."

Something flashed in his eyes as if he already regretted his decision, but he said nothing.

I took the papers and shook his hand. Our palms stayed connected a little longer than they needed to, but I felt unable to let go right away and for that matter so did he.

Christian pulled away and cleared his throat before gathering up some paperwork. "I'll see you in the morning," I said with a big smile. "Thanks again for the opportunity."

Christian nodded distantly, and I could tell it was the end of the conversation. That was all I would be getting out of him. "Well, I'll show myself out, then. Goodbye, Christian," I called as I walked out of his office. I walked into the warm sunlight feeling excited and optimistic.

Things were going to work out great, I could feel it.

Chapter Four

CHRISTIAN

I watched Hannah's annoyingly hot body as she walked to her car. The shape of her ass wrapped in that form fitting skirt was a problem. She looked like a feast waiting to be devoured. My eyes wouldn't—if I was being honest, couldn't—leave her body the entire time. For fuck's sake, I might just have a permanent goddamn boner with her around.

She was hot in all the right ways. Tall and curvy with long, blonde hair that flowed down to her ample chest. And those eyes. Baby blue. I wanted them trained on me while I ran my hands over her body. I caught the way she stared at me when she thought I didn't notice. She wanted me as much as I wanted her.

What the hell am I thinking?

I groaned as I watched her pull away with a satisfied smile on her face.

I hadn't even meant to hire her! I knew she was trouble the

moment I set eyes on her and the play was to pretend to look at her credentials then politely look up and tell her she would be compensated for her time and travel costs, but she was not the right candidate. One minute I was still looking over her credentials, the next I looked into her eyes and before I knew it—the words fell from my lips that she could start tomorrow. Something told me this was a huge mistake. If I couldn't focus now, how much worse would it get when I was around her all of the time?

"She's just a woman and you're not a fucking animal," I whispered to myself.

I'd been around plenty of hot women and some of them were out of bounds, so I knew better than to go there. Hannah Gray was strictly out of bounds. I would just have to control myself. As simple as that. Anyway, the way Annie reacted to her, I wouldn't be surprised if she was gone a lot sooner than she was expecting.

Hmmm. Maybe I could pursue her then...

The thought made my cock stir. It had been way too long since I'd had anyone who'd affected me this strongly. I took the stairs two at a time and stopped off to check on Annie. She was still occupied with her game so I made a beeline for my bedroom. I couldn't understand why I couldn't stop thinking about Hannah Gray, but I had to get her out of my head before I lost my mind.

As I walked into the en-suite bathroom, I tugged my clothes off and tossed them to the side. Then I started up the shower. *A cold shower should do the trick. Fuck!* The freezing water was a shock to my system. My erection died a quick death. I turned the water back to warm. The change was delicious. I leaned my forehead against the tiles and let the water run down my head and back.

Instantly, Hannah Gray slipped into my mind. I saw her sitting in front of me again. Swallowing hard, her pale fingers fidgeting nervously with the strap of her purse. She was perfect. In every way.

The white blouse she'd worn was light and I could make out the faintest hint of a sky-blue bra underneath. She'd adjusted the blouse and tugged up the undershirt cutting off my mesmerizing view, but I could see it even now.

My tongue darted over my lips. The way she pressed her thighs together or toyed with her hair fucking tore me up. Did she even know she did those insufferably sexy things? Those blue eyes looked at me and practically screamed *fuck me.* I had a feeling if I climbed on top of her, she wouldn't mind at all. That just made every nerve more alive and every inch of me long to touch her.

Grabbing the body wash, I started to lather up my skin.

I closed my eyes as my hands drifted over my cock.

My brain conjured up images of her sitting on my desk with those black heels on and nothing more. I wanted to have her prop her feet up on my desk chair... to feel those hot blue eyes on me as I ran my hands down her thighs, gripped them, and pried them apart. I wanted to devour her until she screamed.

But she didn't allow me to. I saw Hannah bend over my desk, her ass in the air as she hiked that skirt up and over smooth, creamy flesh.

My hand turned into a fist as I gripped my length.

I imagined her legs spreading wider for me while she reached back and held herself open for my perusal. That thought alone shot a shiver down my spine. I felt my tongue lick all the way up that wet, pink slit.

The thought of Hannah moaning, squirming and crying out my name was too damn much. My breath caught in my throat and I grunted as I braced my hand against the shower wall and stroked my cock harder.

I threw my head back as my breath came out in little pants. My shoulders juddered as my stomach clenched and tightened. I thought about my bare cock plunging into her body and that tipped me right over the edge. My hips jerked and twitched until I'd pumped every last drop of cum from my body. By the time I was done, I was panting and shaking my head.

What the fuck?

The woman hadn't even started and already—I had fucked her in my head. Just the thought of that supple young body of hers sent shivers up and down my spine. Even after a climax like that, I was still on fire.

Not liking the implication of her effect on me, I quickly rinsed myself off and yanked down my towel before getting out of the shower. I had to stop thinking about her. That was the only way to curb the strong urges that threatened to rear their ugly heads again.

With great deliberation, I pushed Hannah out of my mind as I dried off. I didn't have time in my life for women at the moment. The only person I had time for was Annie. I had to keep my eyes on that and not fall into that honey trap again. The last thing I needed was another Daphne.

Chapter Five

HANNAH

Betsy and I made it home safely. I sailed into my apartment and plopped down on my couch. I felt strangely exhilarated and pumped up on adrenaline as if I'd just got off one of those giant rollercoaster rides.

I kicked off my shoes and leaned my head back against the couch. For the millionth time, I replayed the interview. Christian had been distant, but not cruel. I'd met my fair share of snobby, uptight parents, but that didn't seem to be the problem with him. He just seemed a bit... cold. Not with Annie though, that was warm and natural, and much more important. I'd seen cold parents with their children. Not fun. Those kids were always a little screwed up and who could blame them?

Maybe he just had strict rules about fraternizing with the staff. I one-hundred percent intended to keep him at a safe distance. Mostly because I didn't want to burn through too many panties.

Even so... Christian's sexy face popped into my head again.

No... he was not stuck up, but he definitely had an air of sophistication about him. I thought about the elegant way he moved while he showed me around his house. Part of me wondered what it would be like to climb into his lap and nibble on his ear while he talked.

His lips looked so inviting. A bit on the plump side and just begging for my own lips to be pressed against them. The way he'd licked his lips was enough to almost push me over the deep end. I imagined that tongue sliding into my folds and tasting me. The thought made me shiver. I wanted to feel him touch me, even just once.

Do NOT have these kinds of thoughts about your boss.

I knew it was wrong, but it felt so, so right. I was fascinated by him. His looks, his strong personality. Something so tightly restrained about him made me want to draw out his wild side. I just knew deep down that this man was a monster in all the best ways. I wanted to see more and get to understand the man behind the chilly wall he'd put up.

Come on, Hannah!

I forced myself to get off of the couch and wander into the kitchen. I needed food. Nothing could be wrong enough that a bit of chicken and slice of apple pie wouldn't cure. I peered into my fridge with a slight frown. Other than the apple pie and leftover chicken, the shelves were nearly bare. Thank God, I'd landed the job.

I hadn't had a job in a couple of weeks. After my last nanny position ended, there had been nothing suitable at the agency so all I could do was sit, wait and be glad that I'd had some meager savings put aside, but it had dwindled quickly. A little loan to a good friend to help pay her medical bills, an emergency car repair, rent, food, bills. It all went so quickly. I promised myself I'd be a little more tight-fisted with my finances from now on.

As soon as I put the chicken in the pan to cook, I heard my phone going off in my purse. My heart pounded. What if he was calling to say he changed his mind about giving me the job?

I fished my phone out and saw that it was Natalie. She was one of my best friends since grade school. She was one of those people I could call for anything and the same went with her, but she'd been working so much lately, we hadn't been able to sit down and actually have a long chat. I missed the sound of her voice.

"What are you doing calling me? Aren't you off somewhere learning to save the world?"

Natalie laughed. "I might be in med school, but the only thing I'm off to is my waitressing job, so I can keep paying for med school. How was your interview?"

"Actually, it went great! I was hired on the spot and I start tomorrow."

"Congrats. I'm so proud of you hon. How's the new boss? Sweet or snob?"

I laughed. Natalie knew how it all worked. I usually loved the parents of my kids, but every once in a while I got stuck with someone horrible.

"He's... hot," I said.

"Hot?" I could *hear* the smile on her lips.

"No, really. He's like six foot five at least, with dark hair and these amazing green eyes. And he's so lean and muscular."

"Muscular?" she interrupted eagerly. "How would you know that? Did you come across him shirtless?"

"Don't be such an ass. I could tell underneath his shirt. And that ass," I crooned.

"Gorgeous?"

"Round and just waiting to be squeezed," I breathed.

"Correct me if I've got the wrong end of the stick, but this is your future boss we're talking about, right?"

"Don't worry, I'm just looking. I have no intention of sleeping with my boss."

"Wouldn't it be nice if both of you got off together, fell in love, and lived happily ever after?"

"You've been watching romance movies again, haven't you?" I teased. "I keep telling you that's not how real life works."

"It can and it will," she argued. "Besides, no one knows what's going to happen in the future, so don't be so quick to knock it."

I rolled my eyes. "There's no way in hell, Nat. I know that for a fact. I think he likes to keep a very clear line between him and his staff. I mean it was pretty clear from the way he put up a wall so hard and fast that he wants nothing to do with me in the biblical sense."

"So you thought he was really hot?"

I turned the chicken over. "Oh, my God, yes."

“Did you show him that you thought he was fuckable?”

“Of course not,” I denied immediately. “I’m a professional.”

“Well, then he could have just been acting professional too. Did you see him check you out?"

I thought about it. More than once, I thought I'd saw him looking me up and down. That hunger that rested behind his eyes for a split second was alluring, but it was gone just as quickly as it flashed in those green orbs.

“He did, didn’t he?” she pounced.

"I mean once or twice, but after that he barely looked at me at all. Like I said, there's no way. Besides, I'm okay with that. He's my boss. The last thing I need to do is get tangled up in some kind of romantic tryst and ruin my job. Just before you called, I was staring at an empty fridge."

"I get it," Nat said as I heard her start up her car. “You do need to put yourself out there again though. Just because your ex was a piece of shit doesn’t mean you shouldn’t try again.”

I started peeling the cling-film from the pie. “I’m trying to be sensible and responsible here.”

“And I’m trying to make sure you don’t end up as an old woman with fifty cats,” she said pointedly.

“You’re the most frustrating person in the world,” I declared and I could practically hear her smiling.

“That’s what I’m always going for. Look, all I’m saying is just be open to the possibility of things. I need to go, I'm about to drive. Call you when I get home?"

"How about after work tomorrow? I want to make sure I get plenty of rest before I start in the morning."

"Sounds like a plan. Talk to you tomorrow. Don't hump your boss. Hold out for the ring on your finger first." She hung up before I could reply.

Chapter Six

HANNAH

I shook my head at my phone. What a pain she was, but I wouldn't change a thing about her. Maybe she was right about the dating thing though. I guess it was time to get over the whole Jack thing and find someone new.

I went back to making my dinner as I pondered that thought. When I was done, I carried my food into the living room and settled down on the couch in front of the TV. It was better to watch some crappy show than to keep thinking about Christian. Especially, when those thoughts eventually skewed off to ones where Christian was naked and on top of me.

I polished off my food, the pie was delicious, then I picked out my outfit for the next day. I wanted to dress more comfortably now, since I'd be running after a small child. I settled on a pair of nice jeans and a maroon davenport cardigan. Underneath I decided on a black, short-sleeved shirt so that I would be comfortable and warm if I needed it.

I felt as if I could break into song like Mary Poppins as I

turned in for the night. I was out like a light as soon as my head touched the pillow and it was only my alarm blaring that woke me up. As if on springs, I jumped out of bed and started my routine. In less than half-an-hour, I was standing in front of the mirror holding a mug of coffee and my bag which held any supplies I might need for the day. Snatching my keys from the side table, I jogged out of the door. I was raring to get to work. I was so upbeat, it felt like the start of something great.

A new job and a new child to take care of. This was what I loved.

I reached Christian's place much faster than I anticipated. It was a force of habit for me to always be on time, but I was nearly an hour early. Never mind, I would just let myself in and make myself a cup of coffee or something, if everyone was still asleep. I hopped out of Betsy and went into the building.

Quietly, I unlocked the door and stepped inside. It seemed quiet and still, but I could smell the aroma of expensive coffee beans brewing. From the notes Mrs. Bennet had left for me in the file, I knew that the maid called Maria who arrived at dawn and left before seven, must have started the percolator before she left. For a moment, I stood undecided in the hallway, then I noticed the bedroom upstairs with the pink sign that said: Annie West Lives Here.

I decided to go upstairs and see if she was awake. Picking up my bag where I had packed a few games and toys, I headed towards her door. Sometimes, just going in and sitting down with a child was the perfect ice breaker when dealing with difficult kids.

As I walked down the corridor toward Annie's room, I froze suddenly.

Christian was standing at the end of it. A towel wrapped around his waist. He adjusted the thermostat, then looked up and saw me. Water dripped down his hard body and landed on the polished wooden floor underneath him. The towel didn't cover a ton and his muscular calves flexed as he shifted. His wet hair stuck to his head before he shook it and water droplets flew in different directions.

I was gaping like a fish out of water, but I almost didn't care because he was staring at me just as hard. Even with all that distance between us, I felt the heat between us and holy hell —I wanted to close that space and push my body up against his. I almost craved his touch. It would be wet, warm, and strong. It would be everything. Fantasy images from last night flooded my head. I swallowed hard, my mouth suddenly dry as he slowly walked closer to me.

My heart hammered in my chest. Every step he took made me want to turn tail and run, yet climb him at the same time. I clenched my fingers into fists as he stopped right in front of me.

Then the illusion shattered. He frowned down at me.

I opened my mouth to apologize, but nothing came out. I felt like such a prize idiot when he walked past me, and disappeared into what I assumed was his bedroom. The door closed a little too hard and I jumped. Was he seriously that pissed off? I didn't mean to catch the great billionaire in his towel. True, I showed up too early again, but did it really warrant such an irritated reaction?

I took a moment to collect myself. As amazing of a sight as it had been, I didn't think it was worth the awkwardness it'd caused on my first day. Hopefully, we could both forget it. Him much sooner than me. I shook my head and lifted it. I wasn't here to ogle him. *I'm here to take care of his daughter. And I really, really needed this job. My fridge needed it too.*

Right, so I couldn't get distracted by a strong jaw, muscular arms and a hard satin looking body that dripped with water. I also needed to stop imagining those strong arms wrapped around me. My skin grew hot and I knew it had to be red. Thinking about him like that made me want to fan myself.

Jesus, what is wrong with me?

I wasn't used to being so drawn to someone so quickly. Every time I thought about Christian, I immediately wanted him to touch me, kiss me, and fuck me until I couldn't stand, speak, or think.

I pushed back my shoulders and headed off to find Annie and see if she was awake. By the time I popped into her room, I'd calmed down. To my surprise, she was sitting on the edge of her bed already dressed for the day with her hair in a strange bun hairstyle. I could tell Christian was trying to do the best he could with it, but it was clear he kind of had no idea at the same time. I grinned inwardly. Even that was cute.

"Hey, Annie," I said cheerfully.

"Didn't anyone teach you to knock?" she asked scornfully.

"Actually, I thought you might be still asleep and I didn't want to wake you," I explained.

Her answer was to reach over and grab her phone. She turned it on and immediately buried herself in it.

"What are you playing?" I asked in my friendliest voice.

She angled her body so her face was even more implacably turned away from me.

I sighed. *Okay, it's not going to be so easy*.

I positioned myself within her line of vision and sat cross-legged on the floor. Then I pulled out the games, puzzles, and toys from my bag and laid them out on the floor.

She didn't lift her head.

I picked my ace card. My box of Legos. With it, I could build a whole dinosaur. I started playing with them, a tried and true method for any child. I expected her to come down and join me.

She completely ignored me.

I continued building. Sooner or later, curiosity would compel her.

Suddenly, the door opened and Christian stood in the doorway. With one look, he sized up the situation. I had made zero progress with his daughter.

"I'm off, sweetie," he announced.

"Daddy, can I come with you?" Annie pleaded.

I noticed she had thrown her phone down as it if it wasn't important at all.

"You know you can't," he said calmly. "Offices are not places for little girls. Anyway, you have to stay here and keep Miss Gray company."

"Why can't she go home to her own house?" she asked sullenly, pushing her lower lip out.

"Because," he said sternly. "Miss Gray is your new nanny. She is staying here to take care of you while I'm at work. Be a good girl today, and make Daddy proud, okay?"

She leaned her cheek on the palm of her hand. "Alright."

He came into the room and kissed the top of her head. "That's my girl."

"Daddy?"

"Yeah?"

"I love you."

"I love you too, honey."

From some inexplicable reason, I felt strangely left out. Like the hungry, cold matchstick girl looking longingly through a window at a scene full of food, warmth and happiness.

He turned towards me suddenly. "You have my number, Hannah?"

I nodded quickly.

"Mrs. Bennet will be around soon, and she'll show you the ropes, but call me if you need anything."

"I will."

"See you later, munchkin. I'll be home early today," he said, before he mussed up her hair and left.

Chapter Seven

HANNAH

As soon as he walked out of the door, Annie reached for her phone again. In seconds, she was so engrossed in it, I might as well not have been there.

"Okay," I said, standing up. "How about some breakfast?"

She didn't budge.

I had to smile at how determined she was to not like me. I went downstairs to work on breakfast for her. The fridge was full to bursting and I found everything easily. As I was about to start cooking, Mrs. Bennet arrived.

She wore a black dress with her gray hair tightly swept back, and she seemed like a no-nonsense type of character.

I passed her all the papers I had signed.

She quickly looked them over to make sure I had done them correctly. After that, she proceeded to show me around while telling me the way things were done. A cleaner would come every day at five in the morning and be out before I got there. Basically, it meant I would be at the house on my own with Annie for the most part.

I made mental notes of everything she said.

She was a very thorough woman and after she was finished, I couldn't think of anything else I needed to ask except what was Annie's favorite food.

"Chicken nuggets with chips with a half a bottle of ketchup poured on it," she said dryly.

I laughed. "Okay."

"There's a couple of bags of them in the freezer. Chef makes them himself with organic ingredients, so they're healthy and you can go ahead and make them for her." She gave me her phone number and left.

I went back to making breakfast for Annie. Once I was done cooking, I put it all on a tray and carried it up to her. "Want to eat?"

Annie looked at the plate of eggs, bacon and toast and went back to playing on her phone.

I pushed the plate toward her a bit and then again, when she didn't respond.

"Come on," I urged. "I know you have to be hungry, and this food smells really good. Just take a few bites and see if you like it. If you don't, I'll find something else for you to eat."

I'd arranged the food into a cute little pattern with the bacon and eggs making a smiley face on the toast.

She looked at the plate and huffed, but then she tentatively reached out and snagged a piece of bacon.

I breathed a sigh of relief when she started nibbling on it. After that, I didn't have to prod her to eat her breakfast. I was pretty sure it was some universal law that a hungry child would eventually eat, no matter how stubborn they were.

As soon as the bacon and toast were all gone, she went right back to ignoring the hell out of me.

I tried to coax her into watching a movie with me, but she took one look at the screen and turned her back on it in favor of her phone.

I watched Frozen on my own. Every time I looked over at her, she seemed to be totally engrossed in her screen. It was very unhealthy for a child her age to be so lost in her phone, but I knew banning her from using it outright at this stage would only make her hate me more.

"Alright," I mumbled. "Why don't I go whip us up some lunch?"

Annie didn't even acknowledge that I'd spoken.

I decided to get her to at least eat downstairs, so she'd have a change of scenery. “Let’s eat downstairs.”

She made a face.

“You can bring your phone with you.”

She dragged herself off the bed and followed behind me, but she took her sweet time.

No matter. Getting downstairs was still a small victory. While I made lunch, she lay on the couch gazing into her phone. I made her favorite food and put a bottle of ketchup on the table.

Reluctantly, she pulled herself from the couch. Mrs. Bennet was not exaggerating about the half a bottle of ketchup she lavished on her food. She ate her meal while staring at the phone.

I said nothing, just quietly ate my meal next to her. Afterwards, I cleaned up, put our plates into the dishwasher, and turned to her. "Hey, why don't we go to the park?" I asked brightly.

"I hate the park," she muttered.

"Right. The sun is shining outside. Shall we just out for a little walk?"

"I'm not allowed to be around people," she said dismissively.

I bit my lip. My last hope was the communal gardens. "How about we pop into the garden downstairs for some fresh air? It's looks so pretty and there's no one around at the moment."

Her refusal was point blank. "No."

We were not leaving the house. *Looks like this will be tougher than I'd thought.* I definitely didn't expect a five-year-old to have so much staying power. Hell, she was more stubborn than I was at her age.

We ended up back in her bedroom. I continued building my dinosaur which was starting to look good and she pretended she wasn't interested in what I was doing, but just once her head turned in my direction. Yes, this faithful dinosaur had never failed me before. I'd just started making the long neck, when we heard the front door.

Annie threw her phone on the bed and rushed out. I followed

behind. She was across the hallway and flinging herself at him before I knew it.

Christian caught her and cuddled her against him. He looked so utterly breathtaking in his suit, smiling as he held his daughter in his arms. "How was it today?"

It looked bad, but I knew all Annie needed was a bit of time. "We had a pretty good day. She ate well and enjoyed her phone for the most part. Maybe tomorrow, we'll try going outside."

Annie didn't bother even looking at me, but Christian seemed like he couldn't look away. I felt my cheeks growing hot under his gaze. Every time that man looked at me, it felt like he could see through me, right into my soul. I felt shattered.

"I'm glad you two got along," he said, hugging a madly wiggling Annie against him.

I smiled at the palpable relief on his face. I realized he'd probably been worried all day that things weren't going well, wondering if his daughter was miserable or if she was happy.

I hadn't done anything other than get her to eat, but at least she was well taken care of and safe. "It was no problem. I'll be back tomorrow bright and early. See you tomorrow, Annie."

Deliberately, I did not take the toys back with me. I gave her a wave before she buried her face in her father's shoulder. *You're going to have to talk to me eventually, kid.*

"Hang on," he called to me.

I stopped.

“Can you give me a few minutes to talk to Miss Gray?” he asked Annie.

She slid down along him until her small feet met the floor.

“Wait for me in the living room, okay?” he asked her gently.

She walked towards the living room without even glancing at me.

"Did she say much today?" he asked me.

"Not really. Mostly, she played on her phone, but don't worry about it. These things can take some time. It's an adjustment, but she'll get there."

"You have a lot of confidence," he stated as we stood in the doorway.

"I don't know if it's confidence. It's more like I have faith that eventually, I can get through to any child as long as I'm patient."

"Well, thank you.”

He leaned forward slightly and I caught a whiff of his cologne. It was so intoxicating I nearly knocked myself out.

"It's a real relief having someone around that knows what they're doing."

"I know what you mean. Every parent is nervous the first day when they leave their child with someone new.”

Was it my imagination or was his eyes hungrily roaming my body? “Have a good night, Christian."

"Goodnight, Hannah."

I smiled and waved before I walked away. Even though I didn't turn back to look at him, I could feel his eyes on me. I felt like I would melt underneath his gaze. When was the last time I'd felt like this? Being around Christian stoked my excitement and made my body react in ways I'd never felt before.

Once the door closed I allowed myself to take a deep breath. Whenever I was around him, all I could think about was his hand on my thigh or his lips on mine. And the more I thought about him, the more I fantasized about the possibilities.

"Okay, calm down," I muttered to myself as I rolled down my window to let in some air.

How the hell did I intend to work for Christian if every time I saw him, I had a million inappropriate thoughts about him? It was starting to feel like more than a silly crush that would fade with familiarity. Problem was it wasn't fading it was growing stronger and stronger.

I sat up a little taller. "He is my boss and I'm his employee. I'm going to be cool, calm and professional. End of story."

That's what I had to focus on... my job and his daughter. Nothing else. Besides, he would be at work most of the time. It wasn't like I would have to see him every second of every day. *Surely,* I could handle that. A hello in the morning and an update on how Annie was in the evening. Then a good night. Yeah, I could do that.

Definitely.

Chapter Eight

HANNAH

A week passed and life with Annie settled into a new dynamic. It was a fun time. By fun, I meant I felt ready to pull my hair out. She didn't ignore me anymore. She just said no... no matter what I asked, then flounced off. My reaction was to smile and ask again, because I wasn't going to give up.

Her reaction would always be just downright against anything I said. If I asked her to put her shoes on, she ignored me and walked around barefoot for ages. If I asked her to put away her toys, she took them all out.

I saw the actions and reactions for what they were.

Small acts of defiance calculated to drive me insane.

I knew she was giving me a hard time on purpose. I'd never had to work so hard to gain a child's trust. In the past, it had always taken a few days at most and then I was their best friend. Not with Annie. I started to lose confidence in my ability. Maybe she would be the exception to the rule and I was about to lose my child whisperer status.

"How was she today?" Christian asked as he came home and sat his briefcase on the kitchen counter.

"Same as usual," I said as I put on a smile. "I don't think she wants much to do with me. Did she like her last nanny?"

Christian shook his head. "Honestly, the last nanny quit after a very short time." He looked at me warily. "I hope you're not going to do the same."

"Of course not," I said as I waved a hand and put the last dish into the washer. I shut it and switched it on before I turned back to look at him. "I was just wondering because it's pretty common for children to have a favorite and not like the new one."

He frowned. "No, she didn't bond with the last girl."

"That's okay. We'll work through it." And I meant it too, because she was a pretty good kid even if she seemed so distant. Smart, independent and when she was with her dad, she was just like any other happy, bouncing child.

I dried my hands off before I gathered up my things.

Annie had decided she wanted to be left alone thirty minutes ago so she was upstairs waiting for her dad to come home.

"Thank you for staying with her," he said as he watched me carefully. "We appreciate it." Christian handed my paycheck to me in an envelope.

I pocketed it. My first paycheck meant I could buy groceries, put gas in my car, and pay my mom back. I was sure she was tired of me calling and asking to borrow more, even if she was sweet about it.

"Annie has a doctor's appointment tomorrow," he said as he loosened his necktie and slowly undid it.

I watched and had to force myself to pay attention to his words and not the pulse beating furiously at his throat as he spoke.

"I need you to take her for me. I've already informed them you'll be bringing her instead of me. It's just a standard checkup, nothing too serious. Make sure she is no longer contagious. Her playschool is closed for summer now anyway, but it would be nice to have the all clear."

I forced myself to stop gawking and nodded. "I can do that. No problem."

Christian slid off his suit jacket and hung it on a chair. "Good."

"I should get going."

Christian looked me over.

I wanted to bite my lip to keep from biting into him. The way he rolled up the sleeves of his white shirt made me want to run my hands over his skin.

He licked his lips in that way of his.

I quickly yanked up my bag and pulled it onto my shoulder. "Have a good night," I called out as I hightailed it out of there.

If he stared at me like that again, I might just lose it and forget that I was supposed to be professional with him. I swiftly slid into my car and let out the breath I'd been holding. The more I was around that man the more I found it hard not to give in to that lustful look in his eyes.

He never said anything though.

As much as I caught his hungry looks, he was never anything more than courteous with me. I'd been almost sure he wasn't interested in me, except for those lingering looks.

Chapter Nine

CHRISTIAN

I watched Hannah leave until she turned the corner. She wasn't very good at hiding what was going through her head. Every time she looked at me, I could practically feel her fucking me with her eyes. The more she was around the harder it was becoming to contain myself. Seeing the way she effortless moved around in my kitchen, like she'd been here forever, made things stir in my gut I'd not felt in a long time. I kept telling myself to stop thinking about her, but that was hard to do when I saw her first thing in the morning and as soon as I got back from work.

Every day, she arrived in the morning upbeat and ready to go. When I came home at night, she was still as energetic and cool even after a full day of dealing with Annie. I knew Annie was not being particularly kind to her, but Hannah still tried her best and it was most impressive. She never complained. In fact, she was always positive, sure that Annie could be won over.

As I walked up the stairs, I thought about Hannah's curvy full ass. What I wouldn't give to see her in a black thong, bent over my desk. It made all the fantasies come back to life with a fiery blaze.

I shook the crazy, impure, wonderful thoughts aside as I traded in my work suit for a pair of sweatpants and a t-shirt.

Then I went to check on Annie.

She popped up when I walked into her room. "Oh Daddy, you're back. I didn't hear you."

"No?"

She grinned. "No. Has Miss Gray gone?"

"Yes."

"Good."

I sat next to her on the bed. "How was your day?"

"It was okay," she said as she sat her phone down.

"What did you do?"

Annie shrugged. "Played my game and watched some cartoons."

"Did you do anything with Miss Gray?"

She shrugged again and went quiet.

I knew that was a no. Whenever I brought Hannah up, she pressed her lips in a thin line and refused to talk about her.

I patted her head. "Give her a chance, hmm? She's really trying to get to know you and she's going to be around for a long time."

She was quiet for a minute. "Can we go swimming?"

Just like that, I knew the conversation about Hannah was over. Once Annie made up her mind, it was almost impossible to change it if she wasn't ready. I decided to let it go for the moment. Hopefully, they would be getting along sooner rather than later. "Yeah, we can do that. Then we're going out to dinner."

"We are?" she asked eagerly.

"Mmm..."

"Yay!" she shouted.

"Go on get your swimsuit and I'll go find mine."

Annie bounced off of the bed with excitement.

As I went to grab my trunks, I knew I couldn't force her to come out of her shell, but I had a feeling Hannah would get to her eventually. She had the kind of personality that was hard to resist. If it had worked on me, I was sure it would work on Annie.

Chapter Ten

HANNAH

I packed my bag into the car before I went back to retrieve Annie. She was upstairs on the floor with one shoe on and the other still sitting five feet away from her. I already knew she didn't want to go to the doctor, but I didn't expect her to be so outspoken about it.

"Can you put on your other shoe, please? I put the first one on for you."

"No," she said as she tapped at the phone screen.

“Well, it’s not going to go on by itself,” I said and aimed a smile at her.

She ignored me.

My head started to hurt. She was the cutest little girl in the world but when she wanted to be cold, man was it freezing. I shook my head and tried a firmer approach. "Annie, seriously we have to go like right now, so we don't miss your appointment. Do you want me to help you put it on?"

"I don't want to go."

"I know you don't, but the doctor is important and they're going to make sure you're doing great. So, let's get that shoe on and get out of here. It'll be nice to get some air."

Annie looked directly at me and glared. "I don't want to go."

"I'm right here. There is no reason to yell," I said trying not to let my eye twitch.

"I'm not going and you can't make me. You're just a nanny. I wish you would go like all the others."

"Well, I'm not leaving like all the others and you have to go to the doctor, so I'm just going to help you put this on." I grabbed the shoe so I could get her finished up and we could go.

As soon as I tried to slide it onto her foot, she shifted onto her knees and crawled away.

I sighed and went after her. "Annie, come on," I pleaded. "If you do this, we'll stop on the way back and get ice cream. How does that sound?"

"I don't want ice cream. I want to stay home."

"Well, unfortunately, that's not an option today," I said as I walked toward her with the shoe.

"I'm not going. You can go by yourself!"

"That's enough," I said evenly. "You know I usually wouldn't make you do anything you didn't want to do, but your dad wants you to go to the doctor and we're going. Now, sit down and put on these shoes," I said firmly.

"I hate you!" she snapped.

"Annie!" I called as she turned and ran out of the room.

"Annie, wait," I shouted, but she was already out of the room.

Before I could chase her, I heard a loud shriek and a thud. I flew out into the hallway and saw her tumble down the last few steps then land at the bottom.

For a minute, we were both silent with shock, then she burst into a loud wail of fear and pain. I ran down the stairs almost tripping and falling myself before I dropped down next to her. My knees banged on the hardwood floors, but I barely felt it as I swiftly examined her body.

I couldn't see any blood or serious injury, so I pulled her into my arms as she sobbed her little heart out.

I buried my head in her hair and cried right along with her. My heart wouldn't stop hammering in my chest. "I'm so sorry," I whispered. "I'm so, so sorry. I shouldn't have pushed you so hard."

I felt horrible. Even if it was an accident, it was always hard to explain to a parent that you were the reason their child was hurt. I knew I had to get her to the doctor, but I felt like if I'd just taken a moment to slow down and take another approach, maybe she wouldn't have fallen.

Her arms wrapped around me and held me tight.

My eyes widened.

I cradled her in my hands and looked her over a second time. No bleeding, no bruises. It was a good thing she hadn't hit her head. I pushed hair out of her face. "Does anything hurt?"

Annie nodded her head lightly and pointed to her knee. "Just right here."

"Let me see it." I pushed up the pant leg of her jeans and examined the mark she had on her knee. It wasn't bad, but it was still there. I picked Annie up and carried her into the kitchen. Once she was comfortable, I grabbed an ice pack and a band aid then walked back over to the table. I quickly wiped my eyes and rubbed Annie's head.

"I'm sorry I was horrible to you," she sniffled as she reached up and wiped her face with her sleeve.

“It’s okay,” I whispered. "I'm going to call your daddy, okay?"

She nodded. "Okay," she whispered quietly as she pressed the ice pack to her knee.

I let her focus on that to distract her while I called her father. My heart was in my throat. I knew he'd be pissed at me for letting his daughter get hurt. Everything about Christian screamed overprotective parent and I was sure I would never hear the end of it, but I couldn't blame him one bit for it either.

"Is everything okay?" he asked as soon as answered the phone.

"Kind of," I said slowly before I rushed through what happened. "Annie fell down the stairs. I checked her and I think she's okay, but her knee is hurting. She skinned it a little."

"Take her to the hospital," he said the panic rising in his voice. "They still need to make sure she hasn't hit her head or anything."

I nodded. "I'll take her right now. We'll meet you there."

I ran upstairs and retrieved Annie's shoe before I jogged back down and put it on her. She held out her arms and I picked her up.

As soon as she was in my arms, she laid her head against me and nuzzled against my body.

I carried her outside and made sure she was buckled into her seat before I slid into mine.

As soon as we arrived at the hospital, we were seen. I sat next to Annie the whole time as the doctor started checking her out to make sure that she was okay.

Christian exploded into the room a moment later, his hair tousled, and his eyes wildly searching for his daughter. "Honey, are you okay?" he asked as he arrived at her side

Of course, the minute he asked she started crying again.

I moved out of the way, so they could have some space.

The doctor cleared his throat. "Well, everything looks good. No stitches needed, no concussion, no broken bones. She'll have a little bruise on her knee, but that will fade. Other than that, she looks great. I think she scared herself more than anything. You can take her home."

Christian and I sighed at the same time.

The doctor left the room,

Christian turned to me.

I glanced up at him and steadied myself for the reprimand.

"Thank you for bringing her," he said. "I'm glad it's not too serious."

"I am too. I'm sorry it happened in the first place. I never meant for her to get hurt. Not in a million years."

"I know," Christian said as he looked at me with soft eyes for once. "Accidents happen and little Miss Fussy Pants here can be a clumsy little thing sometimes."

Annie hopped off of the table and wrapped her arms around my legs.

I reached down and smoothed her hair. I hated that it took something so drastic to bring us together, but having her so close made me smile. Annie wouldn't let go of me as we walked out of the room.

"Hannah," Christian said grabbing my attention. "It's been a long day. Why don't you stay for dinner tonight?"

I smiled and looked down at Annie. "Is that okay with you?"

She nodded, and of course, I accepted. We walked out to the parking lot and we all got into the car I was supposed to use for transporting Annie around since Gary, Christian's driver was nowhere to be seen.

"I panicked," he admitted sheepishly after he'd made sure Annie was snapped into her seat. "I was in a meeting when you called and I didn't want to wait for Gary to bring the car around."

I laughed nervously. "Don't worry. You weren't the only one that panicked. My eyes are probably all red and puffy still."

Christian touched my chin.

I stared at him with wide eyes.

He turned my head this way and that, while his fingertips lingered on my skin.

A sudden, pleasant warmth burned through me until it threatened to consume every inch of my body.

"Your eyes are fine," he pronounced finally as he released my chin. "You look just fine."

I felt that familiar warmth slink over my skin as I got into the car and started it. I tried to stay focused on the road. If I didn't I was afraid I'd end up crashing somewhere. Way too many hot thoughts filled my mind and it took everything I had to concentrate on the road.

Christian had never touched me like that before, and part of me was begging for him to do it all over again.

Chapter Eleven

HANNAH

I could smell the aroma of the food as it wafted up the stairs. Instead of ordering in, Christian had insisted on cooking for us. I didn't mind. I didn't know if we would be eating burnt food, but dining with Christian was a treat I never imagined having. Anyway, with the relief and gratitude I felt that Annie was unhurt I would quite happily have eaten ash.

I had carried Annie up to her room and placed her on the bed. Now that she was back home, she seemed to perk right up. "Shall we play together?" she asked.

This was one for the books. She'd never shown the least sign of wanting to play with me.

"Sure. What do you want to play with?" I asked looking at all the toys that were scattered around one half of her room.

"Let's play with this," she said, going over to the big doll house. It was huge with multiple stories all done in light pink and trimmed in deep purple. It had working lights and a doorbell, even a little music player inside. It was exactly the kind of dollhouse I would have loved when I was a child.

"Wow! It's beautiful," I said as she opened it.

"Yeah! Doesn't it look awesome! Daddy bought it for me when I was really little. It's my favorite thing in the world to play with." She picked up one of the dolls and started taking its clothes off. "Did you have a favorite toy?"

I thought about it. "Well, when I was little, I liked my bike a lot, and of course I had some dolls too. I think my favorite toy was probably my play kitchen though. I used to pretend to cook for hours."

"I have a play kitchen too. If you want you can cook with my stuff."

"Thank you. It will remind me of being a child again."

She began to redress her doll in a different outfit. "Do you like children?"

"Yes, I love little boys and girls."

Annie looked up at me. "Is that why you became a nanny?"

I nodded "It is. I've always wanted to help kids and play games with them all day. I think it's fun."

Annie frowned a little. "Not everyone thinks like that though. I... some nannies didn't like me very much."

"I can't imagine why. You are a little darling."

"I guess it was because I was mean to them."

For someone who knew how to drive me crazy on a daily basis I could see there was a lot more to her than I'd originally thought. She was a bright girl even if she was a little lonely and isolated at times.

“I don't think you're mean,” I said. “I think sometimes you just have bad days just like the rest of us. There's nothing wrong with having a bad day. You just have to remember to still treat other people nicely. That's all.”

Annie nodded, her face serious.

“How come your friends don't ever come over?” I asked.

Annie shrugged. “I don't like them to come over.”

“Why ever not?” I asked as I picked up one of the dolls and started dressing her in a lavish ball ground with golden shoes. The doll definitely had more money than I did.

“When we had a sleepover, Mandy said I was stuck up because my house was so big. Then the other girls started acting really weird. Now, I don't really want anyone over. I like going over to their houses though.”

I shook my head. Sometimes kids could be so cruel. It wasn't like Annie had any control over her house, her finances, or anything else for that matter. “Well maybe she was just a little jealous,” I said.

Annie shook her head. “She thinks it's weird that I don't have a mommy too. I told her I do have a mommy, she just doesn't live with me. She said I was still weird. We're not friends anymore. Sometimes I miss her though. Even if she's a butt face.”

I choked on a little laugh and tried to hide it. One thing about kids, they were always honest. When they didn't like someone, it really showed.

Annie scrunched up her face and glared at her doll like the girl was standing right in front of her.

“I'm sure there will be plenty of other friends for you to make in the future. And who knows? Maybe Mandy will come around someday. People change as they get older, you know.”

Annie smiled at me. “Do you really think so?”

“Of course,” I said. “We all have to grow up sometime.”

“So you think we could be friends someday?”

“Maybe. But you know what I would do if I were you. I’d just let it be. If she becomes my friend she does, if not, no big deal. I’d just go find other friends instead.”

Annie nodded and slipped her doll into a car. She pushed a convertible across the carpet and I thought about the fact that her dolls also had a nicer car then I did. They were living the life. I chuckled to myself at the thought.

“What are you laughing at?” she asked.

I wouldn’t tell her those thoughts. So, I began to make up a story about the doll in my hand. Annie and I created such a fun story together that I forgot we were even waiting for dinner. I think she forgot too, because when we both looked up Christian stood in the doorway.

How long had he been standing there?

"What are you two doing?" he asked lightly, as the corner of his mouth quirked up into a grin.

"We're playing, thank you very much," I said as I stuck my nose up. "You're interrupting our mystery. We were just about to find out who stole the money from the bank."

Christian raised a brow. "Whose idea was that?"

"I know it was definitely Tina," Annie said as she narrowed her eyes at my doll.

I gasped. "You're throwing me under the bus? I thought we were partners!"

"I don't want to go to jail," Annie stated seriously.

“Neither do I,” I shot back.

Annie burst into a fit of giggles.

I joined her.

I glanced over my shoulder at Christian and sucked in a sharp breath.

He stood there just staring at me. The look in his eyes was soft and appraising like he wanted to say something. Instead, he cleared his throat again and the look faded away. "Dinner is just about ready. I came to get you two so it would still be hot by the time it's done. Ready?"

"Yeah.” I nodded. “We should put the toys up really quickly though. I'm sure someone's going to be exhausted after dinner and bath time."

"Will not," Annie piped up. "I can stay up all night."

"I don't think so," Christian and I said at the same time and we both chuckled.

She pouted at us. "I'm old enough," she insisted. "I want to stay up."

"No way," I said. "I have to watch you in the morning and you're already a big enough grump when you've had your full eight hours. We can however, read a book after dinner before I have to go for the night." I stood up and stretched. My muscles whined at sitting on the floor cross-legged for so long like I was still a child. I started picking up the toys.

"Three books," Annie shot back.

"Two."

"Deal." She grinned.

"I feel like that child just tricked me," I muttered.

I saw Christian stifle a laugh.

Chapter Twelve

HANNAH

Annie and I worked together to put away the rest of the toys while Christian went to check on dinner. When we were done, she slipped off to go and wash her hands and I went downstairs to see if I could help with anything.

"Dinner's served," Christian said looking pleased with himself as he swirled pasta on our plates. Steak sat beside it and fresh steamed broccoli too. He had opened a bottle of red wine and quarter-filled two glasses with it.

"What do you think?" he asked, one eyebrow cocked.

"I think I've died and gone to food heaven. I can't believe you cooked all of this," I exclaimed as I picked up a noodle covered in white sauce and sucked into my mouth. I licked my finger. "This is delicious."

I gazed up as I felt his eyes on me.

He stared at me as if he was in an incredulous daze. Then he swallowed thickly. He shook himself out of his strange state immediately, but that heated look stayed in his eyes.

If not for Annie coming down and climbing into her seat at the table, I don't know what would have happened. She kicked her feet happily, as Christian put a plate in front of her and a cup of juice. "Can I have ketchup, please?" Annie asked.

"No," I was happy to hear her father say very firmly.

"Awww," she grumbled, but she didn't protest beyond that.

Hiding a smile, I settled in at the table and we all started eating. Even with Annie there chattering away, it was odd, the tension that flowed between the two of us. Every time he looked at me, I could feel his eyes as if they had stripped me naked and were appraising every inch of my body.

I had downed three glasses of wine by the time dinner was done. I couldn't help it. Every time I looked at him, I became a ball of nerves and desire that I couldn't even explain. I dabbed at my mouth with a napkin and looked over at Annie to distract myself.

She was an absolute mess.

"Were you trying to eat your dinner, or wear it?" Christian asked her.

Annie grinned. "I tried to eat it, but it was as slippery as worms."

"I think you just like making a mess." I laughed as I cleaned up her face and hands as best I could. "Let's get you into a bath and then into bed. Then you can say goodnight to your daddy."

Annie held up her arms.

Christian picked her up and hugged her as she kissed his face. He pulled a face as she left behind a mess of pasta sauce.

I laughed so hard at the OCD businessman's disgusted expression that my stomach hurt. "I don't think he likes messes all that much," I teased.

"I don't like being slobbered on," he corrected.

"You love it!" Annie laughed as she covered his cheek in wet, messy kisses.

I finally rescued him by taking her into my arms. "Don't give your daddy such a hard time. He made us a delicious dinner."

Her little arms went around my neck. "No more slobber kisses for Daddy."

"No more," I agreed.

"I appreciate that," he said, and leaned over to give her a kiss on her cheek.

As soon as he did, I could smell his cologne. It was subtle and spicy and made me want to smell it more. I felt a jolt travel up my spine. He glanced at me and for a moment, I wished he'd kiss my cheek too. I had the smallest desire to be part of this family. To be the one to wake up with them, be with them, play with them and grow with them.

You're getting way too attached.

"I'll be up in a minute for story time," Christian said, but his voice sounded strangely husky.

"See you in a minute," Annie sang.

I turned on my heels quickly. Annie and I had a minimally splashy bath time which I was happy for. Usually, Annie could cover the whole floor in water at one time. Usually, when I turned around to grab a toy or a towel she would splash as much water as she could. At the moment, she seemed content to play with her mermaid and ducks. When I said it was time to leave, she happily stood up and let me swaddle her in a towel before I carried her into her bedroom. It felt good to carry her, because usually, she didn't want to be touched by me.

"Which PJ's do you want to wear?"

I'd noticed a long time ago that she got excited when it was time to pick a pair out for herself. Of course, she'd never told me which she liked before, but tonight she talked my ear off. It was actually a surprisingly welcome change. I didn't realize how much it had affected me that I couldn't get her to open up to me.

Christian came up during story time and shared the reading with me. By the time the story was done, Annie was out. She was curled up around her stuffed bear, her long hair spread on the pillow as she smiled even in her sleep.

"She's so adorable..." I sighed. "I always knew we'd get along if she just gave me a chance."

"Yeah. I'm glad she decided to go easy on you. She could use a friend when I'm not around." He glanced at his watch.

"I'll clean up the kitchen before I go," I said quickly. It had been a wonderful night so far and I didn't want any awkwardness to start now.

“You don't have to. The maid will do it in the morning.”

“No, it will be all crusty by the morning and much harder for her. I don't mind and it's only fair. You slaved over a hot stove for us."

"I'll help you," Christian said as he kissed Annie's head and stood.

He followed me out of the room into the kitchen.

We rolled up our sleeves and smiled at each other. It felt comfortable to be doing this. Like a piece of domestic happiness, I had always dreamed about. The place wasn't overly messy because he must have done some cleaning while he cooked. I grabbed a towel when the dishwasher stopped and began to dry the contents.

Quiet reigned for a minute before he glanced at me. "Thank you," he said, turning to me.

"For what?"

"For taking such good care of Annie."

"Hmm... I let her fall down the stairs," I said, as the very thought of it made me cringe. "I still feel awful about that."

"That's how I know you care about her. Also, you thought on your feet in a crisis situation and I like that. So really, you are doing a great job with her."

"I'm trying. She's a good kid and I have a lot of patience for her."

"Clearly..." He nodded. "I wasn't totally honest before."

"About what?"

"About the amount of nannies she's had. She's had a ton of them over the last year. She didn't like any of them and found a way to make all of them quit."

"Why didn't you tell me?"

He put the cutlery away in the drawer as he explained, "I thought if you knew that you'd get discouraged and not want to stick around. People love to take the easy route. A difficult child is more often than not looked at as if they're bad, and there's nothing else to them. I don't think a child should have to be perfect to be loved. She's going through a hard time, but she's not a bad kid."

"I think the same thing as you. I was a little worried there that we would never get along, but I'm glad she's warming up to me. She's hilarious." I grinned as I thought about us playing.

"Did you ever think about leaving?"

I glanced up at him. His voice had changed and the look on his face was part concerned and part something I couldn't begin to decipher. I touched his arm. It was an instinctive gesture. "Not once. I told you in the beginning that I don't give up. I wouldn't do that to either of you."

Christian took in a deep breath. His eyes slid down to my hand that lingered on his muscled arm.

I pulled my hand back when I realized what I was doing. His gaze flicked up to mine and immediately I wished he would push me against the counter and rip my clothes off. My breathing picked up as he let his hand slide down and linger on my hip. It was the smallest touch, but it radiated desire and longing.

Fuck.

Every thought that went through my head was dirtier than

the last. My eyes were drawn to his inviting lips. When he licked his sensuous bottom lip, I shuddered. "What are we doing?" I asked quietly.

"I just wanted to say thank you. That's all," he said in a deep, husky voice.

Just the sound of that voice made my knees weak.

Christian's hand shifted from my hip and he turned towards the table again.

I could see the tension in his body and his reaction to me pushing so hard against the fabric of his pants and it was an impressive push too. I wanted to press my hand against it, slide it against my lips and watch him moan as he gave into me.

I swallowed hard. My entire body felt hot and bothered, so I had to force myself to breathe right again.

We finished cleaning up and put everything away in relative silence only making small talk after that. I don't think either of us could really focus.

"Would you like me to drive you home?" Christian asked when we were done. "You've had a couple of glasses of wine."

"Oh yeah, I have." I laughed lightly. I hoped that was why I felt so damned hot and flushed. "What about Annie though?"

"I'll ask Gary to come over and keep an ear out for her. He'll probably be in the pub around the corner." He smiled.

I smiled too and shook my head. "Sounds like a plan. Let me grab my things."

"I'll wait for you here," he said, already speed-dialing Gary.

I nodded and jogged upstairs to grab the bag I'd left in the spare room. I hadn't wanted to wake Annie up when I came back to retrieve it. Slowly, I pushed her bedroom door open a bit. I saw her still passed out and I smiled with satisfaction.

"Night kid."

I snagged my bag, and stopped very briefly to check that I looked okay in the en-suite bathroom mirror then walked out to the living room where Christian was waiting on me. Gary must have sprinted down the road because he was already nestled on the couch and polishing off the rest of the wine bottle.

I climbed into his gleaming sports car and Christian closed the door down after me.

"Ready?" he asked.

I nodded. As he pulled away from his home, I had a thought of staying the night and waking up there.

You're getting ahead of yourself, madam.

I knew I was, but my imagination had a mind of its own sometimes. I couldn't stop it even if I wanted to.

Chapter Thirteen

HANNAH

The drive back throbbed with the sound of the engine and something else mysterious that seemed to hang in the air between us. The overhead streetlights flooded the interior of the car and every once in a while with enough light, I could dart a look in his direction to check out his expression.

Christian's hands gripped the wheel so hard his knuckles were white. His lips seemed to move silently as if he were having some kind of inner dialogue.

I would have killed to know what he was murmuring. I had a sneaking suspicion it might be the same thing that was in my head.

Every ounce of tension that flowed off his body made me just as anxious and antsy as he seemed to be. I wanted to ask him what was going through his head, but I didn't dare. I wasn't sure what I'd say if he said he wanted to throw me down and have his way with me.

I shoved my thighs together and squeezed as my fingers gripped the seat tightly.

Calm down, Hannah. There is absolutely no way that anything is going to happen between us.

It couldn't. He was my boss, my employer. If I crossed that line, I'd be potentially screwing up a job that I really liked and wanted to keep. Plus, I'd just made a huge breakthrough with Annie and I didn't want to throw it away. I couldn't risk that. Right?

The car pulled up to my apartment building and I glanced around. The parking lot looked pretty empty. I was very aware that we were completely alone in the luxurious, but tight confines of his car.

I swallowed and turned to him. "Thanks for the ride," I said. I had tried to make it sound light and casual, but even to my own ears, it sounded like I was ready to rip his clothes off and jump him. Our eyes locked and for once, neither of us turned away. I drowned in the depths of his lust filled- hooded green eyes. I tried to think of something to say to him, but my mind churned uselessly and came up with nothing.

Christian shifted in his seat and captured my lips without a word.

His mouth was hot against mine. Heat and passion locked onto me as I melted in my seat. His hands gripped my face and pulled me closer. Any reluctance I might have had shattered and all the longing I had felt since the day I met him exploded out of me and poured over us.

I pushed my hand against his cheek and felt the rough stubble beneath my palm. The way it grated against my skin only turned me on even more. My lips parted and my tongue darted out to taste him. His tongue slid along mine and I trembled in his arms.

Our kiss went from exploring and passionate to deep and fevered. Moans filled the car, our chests heaved, and the panting sound of our breaths made my toes curl.

Christian's hand slipped underneath the fabric of my shirt. His fingers moved over my chest, down to my bra. He shoved it up and his fingers caressed my already hardened nipples.

I gasped against his mouth and felt the wetness flooding between my thighs. "Christian," I whispered against his mouth.

“Fuck, you taste so amazing,” he muttered hoarsely, as his fingers threaded into my hair. He pulled me closer, his tongue quick and eager as he pinched my nipples one after the other.

I rocked against my seat as my pussy screamed for more friction. I needed to feel more. I needed to feel everything. I shifted in my seat and in the small confines managed to straddle Christian's lap. The length of his rock-hard cock pressed up against my wet panties. His face showed surprise until I ground myself against his cock. He attacked my mouth with fervor as his hands gripped my rounded ass.

"Hell," he growled. "I want you like I’ve never wanted another woman."

"I want you too," I panted. "So bad.

“I can’t sleep at night," he admitted.

Well, I couldn't think straight, couldn't even speak, as I was consumed by his kiss and his touch. His strong hands hiked up my skirt and exposed my thighs to the cool air of the AC. He gripped my thighs and they burned up where he touched. I felt myself trembling in his hands.

My breath caught in my throat as his fingers pushed between my thighs. I cried out as I felt the tip of his finger rub around my clit and stroke the sensitive flesh through my panties. My hips jerked toward him and rubbed against that finger, begging for more of that amazing sensation. As he kissed the line of my throat to my shoulder and collarbone, his finger circled my clit like a dog chasing its own tail. Again and again. Round and round. Faster and faster.

"More," I moaned against his mouth. "Give me more."

Christian grunted and pushing aside the fabric of my panties, rubbed directly against my clit. His fingers slid through my wetness and he used it to coat his fingers before he slipped a thick digit inside of me.

I gasped, his name on my lips, as my head tilted back with my eyes closed and rolling back in pure pleasure.

He worked his finger in and out until I couldn't breathe.

I rotated my hips as I tried to draw out more of that torturous sweet pleasure but it wasn't enough. Christian pushed another inside of me then another until his fingers pushed and prodded, opening me up and stretching me wide for him.

"Christian, slow down," I panted. "I'm gonna climax if you keep doing that."

"Come for me," he growled, as his fingers picked up speed.

They curled and prodded my sensitive spot until I couldn't breathe.

"Come," he ordered.

I buried my face in his neck and my body trembled all over as I felt the orgasm build in my belly until my body tensed and went completely still. I cried out, my teeth sank into his flesh and my nails buried in his skin as I held on for dear life. Color burst behind my lids as every inch of me was overwhelmed with sheer unadulterated pleasure. The orgasm took over as I jerked and spasmed on top of him until it ebbed away and my body went limp. I was left spent and panting against his hard body.

I heard him breathing fast and shallow in my ear as he pulled his fingers free. I heard the sucking sound of wetness before I forced myself to open my eyes. Just in time to see Christian licking his fingers clean, the look of pure lust in his eyes was enough to make me want to rip his pants off and fuck him in the front seat of his car.

He caught me watching and licked slowly as if he was luxuriating in the taste of me.

"Fuck..." I breathed.

It was bad enough that he was so damn sexy but for him to be that openly dirty? It wasn't fair. I felt as if the universe was trying to conspire against me. His hand gripped my ass and squeezed bringing me back to life. I glanced around the parking lot. Heck, I'd completely forgotten where we were.

Out of the corner of my eye, I spotted a familiar figure. She was walking from the apartment buildings and headed in our direction. I groaned. My nosey neighbor Katherine. I quickly pulled myself off of his lap and settled myself back into the passenger seat even as I tugged down my skirt and adjusted my soaked panties.

"Shit. That's my nosey neighbor. I hope she didn't see anything," I muttered to myself.

Katherine loved to gossip. Anything she found out about her neighbors would be known to the entire apartment building in no time. By now, everyone was well aware to avoid her like the plague at all costs.

I fixed my hair and felt the loose strands on my shoulders before I swept them back up into a ponytail. "I should go," I said quietly.

Christian nodded. I glanced at him fully, but his attention was in front of him and no longer on me at all. It made my stomach drop a little bit and I didn't know why. It's not like we'd even had sex. Still, I could feel that cold side of him coming off in waves. He was going right back to the way he was before. What the hell was that about? Did he regret what we did?

It was silly, something that wasn't in the least bit important. I tried to convince myself of that, but I knew that even after that quick session of fooling around that I wanted him desperately. I would have let him upstairs, but I knew he had to get home to Annie.

"I'll see you tomorrow," I said tentatively.

"Yeah," he grunted and adjusted his pants. "See you tomorrow."

I slipped out of the car and bit my lip. Was he mad because we had to stop there and he didn't get his turn? I couldn't imagine him throwing a fit over not getting some pussy. Someone like him, he could get it anywhere and anytime. I doubted he needed me to get off. I watched him roar out of the parking lot before Katherine reached me.

"Well, well, that's some car," she said.

I knew she was dying of curiosity. "Nice, isn't it? Anyway, good night, Katherine," I said, before turning away and walking towards my apartment.

Why did it feel like I'd just made a huge mistake?

Chapter Fourteen

CHRISTIAN

What the fuck was I thinking?

I stared at the ceiling and wondered what exactly had happened to my last brain cell to make me fool around with Annie's nanny. The first one she actually liked.

Seeing them together had made my heart swell with happiness that finally my daughter had found someone she liked, but it had also made me want Hannah Gray more than anything.

My craving for her wouldn't calm down. I wanted her on top of me desperately. Hell, I hadn't fooled around in a car since I was a teenager. She'd rocketed me back to those times when life was easy and carefree. I thought about her cheeks becoming rosy and the way she gasped when my fingers slipped inside of her. I closed my eyes and imagined the way it felt when her tight pussy clenched around my digits. I heard her moaning my name and immediately felt my cock stiffen.

It was still early in the morning. I knew she'd be in before Annie woke up, so I had a little time to myself. I fisted my cock and pumped it as I thought about her. Hannah's smooth skin, her angelic voice, her soft tits as she'd bounced against me.

I stroked myself until her name was a prayer on my lips. Her sea blue eyes urged me on. I swore I could still taste her on my lips, still smell her on my skin.

"Fuck, Hannah," I whispered.

My back arched as my fist tightened and I thought about her soft lips on mine, the scent of her as she came, the flavor of her on my lips. She was perfect. She stirred up things inside of me I didn't know existed.

The sound of the front door closing brought me back to reality.

"Hannah," I whispered.

I always knew when it was Hannah. She liked to hum first thing in the morning, usually whatever was on the radio on her way in. That soft sound drifted upstairs and permeated my door as she walked up and came closer to my room. I listened to the footsteps and thought about her coming into my room saying she wanted me as my cock swelled even more and filled my palm.

Before she could take her clothes off in my mind, I had come hard and fast, my body convulsing with intense need, my cum shooting out of me violently.

It was silent outside my door. I wiped myself with some tissue paper, scrambled out of bed, and made a beeline for the bathroom. Chucking the tissue into the toilet, I stood at the bathroom sink and looked at myself in the mirror. There was something different about me. My eyes looked almost haunted. It looked the way I felt—restless and dissatisfied. The hunger for her was like a disease eating me up from the inside.

"Fuck, this is getting worse," I swore angrily."Don't fuck the fucking nanny. Is that so hard?"

I thought I could purge her out of my system by masturbating, but that was just making it worse. I turned on the tap with a vicious movement. In the shower, brushing my teeth, shaving and brushing my hair, I thought about her. Her damn humming kept playing in the back of my mind. Like it was on a fucking loop.

I grabbed my things and headed downstairs for a quick cup of coffee. It had already brewed and filled the house with its aroma when I walked into the kitchen.

Hannah glanced at me then her eyes darted away quickly. "Morning," she said quietly. It was clear she wasn't happy about what happened last night either.

"Morning," I grunted out.

Usually, she smiled at me every morning and we'd chat a little before work. Today, she was closed off and she busied herself by taking out activities that she'd planned to do with Annie and laying them on the table.

I took a gulp of my coffee and burned my tongue, which made my temper even fouler.

"Anything I should know for today?" she asked without looking at me. "Appointments?"

"No," I answered shortly, putting my cup on the counter.

I felt her eyes on me as I headed out of the kitchen. There was nothing else to be said between us. She knew how to look after Annie and if she needed anything, she could text me. If she felt too pissed about the night before, she'd quit and that would be the end of that. Maybe that would be a good thing. It would stop the torture for me.

It wouldn’t be the best thing for Annie though.

Chapter Fifteen

HANNAH

Oh, my God! I knew it would end up being weird.

I watched Christian's retreating back and it told me everything I needed to know. He regretted what we'd done and he was obviously irritated with me. After all, I started it. I hated the feeling in the pit of my stomach. There was no denying it... I cared what he thought and it wasn't going away either.

I shouldn't have fooled around with him.

But I didn't expect Christian to go back to being so cold to me right after we'd gone up in flames like that. I thought about his hands on my body, the feeling of his breath against my skin and his cock pressed up against my body until all I could think about was riding him.

"Morning!"

I snapped out of my daydream so quick, I damn near gave myself whiplash.

Annie stood in the doorway in her PJ's and her bare feet as she snuggled one of her dolls to her chest.

I smiled at her and her face lit up.

"Good morning," I said cheerfully, putting Christian firmly out of my head. "I hope you're ready to have a lot of fun because I've got games, coloring books, dolls and we're going swimming."

Her mouth dropped open. "We're doing all of that today?"

"Sure are. Let's have a whole day of adventures. Soon, you'll have to go back to school."

Annie cheered as she ran from the room and back up the stairs.

I grinned and followed her. Annie and stairs were still a source of nervous energy for me. I knew she could walk them and run them, she had many times before, but seeing her land at the bottom of the stairs was still fresh in my mind.

I helped her find an outfit for the day. She decided on a pair of soft, peach shorts and a white tank top with *Princess* emblazoned across the chest. Then I brushed her hair, braided it into a French braid so she would really look like a Princess. Once we fished out her swimsuit, we headed downstairs for breakfast and games until the sun had time to warm up the day.

Thankfully, Annie seemed to have completely forgotten the traumatic events of the day before. She was in a talking mood and hardly stopped to even take a breath.

I stared at her in amazement. She was like a different child and it seemed strange to me that simply falling had made all the difference. There had to be more, but I couldn't figure out what.

We had a wonderful day. We swam and played by the poolside under the morning sun, then still dressed in our swimsuits, she helped me cook and clean while she chatted my ear off. After lunch and a short rest, we went back into the water. It was nearly four when we came back upstairs. I put on the music and we danced like mad savages. It was fun and by the time we stopped we were both panting.

I planned to take off when Christian came home, but Annie was already asking me to stay for dinner. As much as I wanted to hang out with her more, I knew I shouldn't stick around. Not tonight.

"Please?" Annie pleaded. "Daddy will make something good for us to eat and we can stay up late because it's Friday! Please, please, *please?*" she begged.

"You're a persistent little thing when you want to be," I stated with a grin as I dried off the dishes and placed them into the cabinet. "But maybe not tonight, Annie."

Annie responded by whining and pouting. I knew she didn't mean to be a brat, but she was lonely as hell. She wrapped her arms around my waist and laid her head on my stomach as she pleaded again.

"What's going on?" Christian asked as he stepped into the kitchen.

Wow, he was back early. Thank God, I had slipped my robe over my bikini.

"Daddy!" Annie yelled as she released me and wrapped

herself around his waist instead. "We played games and we went swimming and we danced and... and..."

"Oh, yeah?" Christian encouraged. He had no problem listening to Annie's plethora of updates about our day. Instead of being irritated the way I'd seen some busy, high-powered parents get, he always smiled indulgently and paid her his full attention. Often asking her questions and laughing at the silly jokes she'd told until she would wear herself out and simply hug him tightly.

"Can Hannah stay for dinner tonight?" she asked eagerly.

"Annie," I said wearily. "I told you that it wouldn't be a good idea tonight. Maybe another time."

Annie pouted and I watched her little cheeks turn red. I could see her about to lose it, but I gave her a little look and she quickly stopped. As much as I adored her, the tantrum wasn't going to get me to stay. I wouldn't reward that behavior and she knew it.

"Please," she begged.

"You could stay if you wanted," Christian said quietly. "We're not doing anything and it wouldn't take me too long to whip up a meal for us."

I chewed my lip indecisively. Christian's expression had softened since the morning, and I couldn't stand the sound of Annie begging me for anything. I wanted to see her smile, not make her miserable. I slung the towel in my hand over my shoulder. "Okay, okay, I'll stay for dinner."

Annie grinned. "Yay!"

I walked over and pinched her nose to make her giggle. "Now

go upstairs and get ready for a shower. We need to get that pool water off of your skin and get you into some proper clothes."

"Can I wear PJ's to dinner?" she asked.

"Ask your father."

Christian seemed to think it over before he shrugged. "I don't see why not... as long as it doesn't become a habit."

"Yes!" she yelled and took off in a flash.

I watched her go before I sighed and shook my head. "That girl is going to make all of my hair gray before its time."

"You're just now discovering that?" Christian asked with a raised brow. "I've been going gray since she was two. Congrats, you get to share in these joyous moments with me now."

I laughed nervously as he laid his briefcase on the table. I hadn't forgotten about the day before and what we did. My laughter died a sudden death and I intentionally busied myself with wiping down the counters. It was better than seeing that cold look in his eyes again.

"Can we talk?" Christian asked quietly.

I glanced up at him.

His face was serious, but it didn't have as hard of an edge. His hands were buried in his pockets as he looked at me curiously.

I laid the towel down and nodded. "Yeah, sure. Why not?" I tried to smile. "What do you want to talk about?"

"I'm sorry about last night. I shouldn't have let things go that far and make you feel uncomfortable about it."

I stared at him. "I thought maybe you were mad at me," I said quietly.

"Mad? No, I enjoyed it. That wasn't the point." He shook his head as if to wake himself up. "I shouldn't have made a move like that and I shouldn't have let it continue. Look, I don't do relationships. Ever. So I'm sorry if I led you on."

I blinked at Christian. *Not ever?* I wanted to ask him so many questions, but instead, I choked it all down. I shouldn't feel any pain, but my stomach dropped and suddenly, I felt horrible. I nodded at him and forced a smile. "Oh, I understand. I'm not that great with relationships either," I said, and tried to shrug it off.

Christian looked like he didn't totally believe me, but I didn't give him time to question it. I mumbled an excuse about changing out of my swimsuit and hustled up the stairs. As soon as I was in the bathroom, I took in a deep, shuddering breath and let it out slowly.

"What did you think would happen?" My voice sounded bitter even to my own ears.

I splashed my face with water and retrieved my bag before I changed. For once, I didn't want to stick around, but I did it anyway for Annie. At least, she would be happy and I would know for sure to put my silly fantasies behind me.

Chapter Sixteen

HANNAH

I rolled over the next morning and groaned. Sunlight beaming onto my face wasn't a good way to wake up, especially when I was slightly hung over. Natalie had showed up with two bottles of wine, a platter of sushi and an insatiable need to gossip and cheer me up. I loved her for it.

Until now.

It took more than a few tries to get out of bed and onto my feet. I staggered into the bathroom and started the shower. As soon as the water touched my skin, I slumped and rested my forehead against the cold tiles.

Christian's face popped into my head and I groaned.

Why can't I stop thinking about him?

Throughout dinner, we'd remained civil, but I didn't look at him, could barely speak to him. It wasn't like I was trying to be unfriendly on purpose, but every time I tried to be normal with him my voice caught in my throat and I couldn't bring myself to further humiliate myself. I'd spent most of the night answering Annie until it was time to go and then I'd disappeared as soon as he started reading to her.

My fingers worked through my tangled hair. I need to just get over it. I had been stupid, but this was the end of the madness. He'd put me in my place in no uncertain terms. I ran a hand over my face as I heard my phone ring. I stayed still like it was a predator and I was its prey. When it stopped, I resumed showering, but the sound reverberated once again, and demanded that I answer it.

I stepped out of the shower dripping water on the bathroom floor as I rushed to the phone. When I grabbed my phone from my bed, Christian's name made me freeze. What could he possibly want? I wished I had the strength to let it go to voicemail, but I couldn't stop myself from answering, "Hello?" I asked tentatively.

"Hey, Hannah," he said sounding relieved. "Are you at home?"

I stared at the phone for a minute. I hadn't missed a day somewhere. It *was* Saturday, right? I checked the lock screen on my phone and it popped up as Saturday, after all. I hadn't expected to hear from him on a weekend. I nestled the phone back against my ear. "Yeah, I'm at home. What's up?"

"Uh, I know you aren't scheduled to be working this weekend, but a commercial came on TV with a tiger exhibit and Annie has decided that she has to go to the zoo today. Right now, she's packing a bag and getting changed into her tiger print PJ's and I don't think she's going to change her mind."

I grinned despite myself. I could already imagine her wrapped in her tiger PJ's with the hood pulled up and one floppy ear that never seemed to want to stand up even after I beefed it up with sticky tape.

"Can you do this today? I'll throw a bonus into your paycheck," Christian coaxed.

A bonus? For going to the zoo with Annie and him on a day when I had nothing else to do but mope around the house. "Yeah," I agreed. "Whatever Annie wants, Annie gets." I laughed to make sure he did not think I was taking a dig at his parenting methods. "Let me get dressed and I'll be over."

"Actually, I thought I could pick you up. We're at the country house so it would be completely out of your way."

The way my head felt? I could definitely use a day without driving. I quickly picked up a bottle of pills and shook two out. "I'll be ready when you get here."

"See you soon."

I took the time to change into a pair of black shorts and a bright pink tank top, just in case Annie wandered off she could find me easily. I pulled my hair into a ponytail high on my head. Annie loved it when I wore my hair that way. Every time she saw it, she got a kick out of it and I always had to do hers the same way.

I was much more excited about the trip than I thought I could be. I was looking out of the window when they pulled up. Christian was not in his blood red Aston Martin, but driving a black BMW. I jogged down the stairs and slipped into the passenger seat.

He was right about one thing, Annie was dressed in her tiger outfit, and she looked darn cute in it.

She growled.

I grinned at her.

Christian looked good too. Much better than good. I didn't see him in casual clothes often, but I loved the way his jeans hugged his body. The casual t-shirt he wore showed off his muscles. I didn't realize I was staring until he glanced at me and I quickly looked away.

"Hannah, look at my shoes," Annie said as she waved and fought her seatbelt until Christian told her to cut it out.

"You have to stay in your seat."

"I want to hug Hannah," she whined.

"You can hug her when we get to the zoo."

"Daddy," she groaned.

"Annie Elizabeth West, I mean it. If you get out of that seat while I'm driving, we won't go."

Annie pouted and crossed her arms over her chest.

I shook my head. How can something so small be so cross?

Christian wouldn't pay her attitude any attention and ten minutes later she'd forgotten that she was even upset as she sang and clapped along to kid's songs on the radio.

"Sorry to drag you out on a Saturday," he said with a sigh. "Usually, it's just us, but she seems to have gotten so attached to you."

I smiled. "I don't mind. Besides, it's not like I was doing anything anyway. And I actually like the zoo."

"Really?" Christian asked.

I nodded. "Are you kidding me? I love the penguin exhibit and the aquarium. Those are my favorites. I'm excited to see the tigers too."

"Did you know tigers only eat meat?" Annie asked excitedly from the backseat as she bounced up and down. "They hunt and eat their prey like this." She proceeded to growl and pretend to tear apart an animal.

I grinned at her with amusement, then glanced over at Christian.

He looked like he was ready to cry from laughing. "And you said I was wrong when I called her weird," he whispered.

"Nope, I see it now. Your child is strange."

"Thank you," he said with pride. "She's a product of yours truly."

"If it was only you, she'd just be awful, not strange," I countered.

Christian jaw dropped with surprise, but I pretended to stare at my phone. I could feel his need to say something to me almost on the tip of his tongue, but he snapped his mouth shut and concentrated on the road.

I chuckled under my breath. So totally worth it.

As soon as we arrived at the zoo, Annie was ready and raring to go.

Christian shouldered a bag he'd stocked supplies into. Probably extra drinks and snacks in case she needed to refuel between food stands.

I'd say he was overprotective, but I'd seen an Annie melt-down. It wasn't pretty.

"Do you want to see the tigers first?" Christian asked her.

"Yes!" Annie chimed up right away. "Tigers and then the aquarium for Hannah."

"Aww... you're so thoughtful," I said.

Annie grinned and held my hand. She reached out and took Christian's hand with the other. We looked over the top of her head as we started walking and our eyes locked. I felt my face heat up as Christian's mouth suddenly tilted into the sweetest smile I'd ever seen.

What the hell is that about?

It took everything in me to turn my head and focus on the walk ahead of us. Even when I did, I could feel the heat in my cheeks. I was pretty sure my face would be the color of a tomato for the entire trip if he continued to be so charming. I should have told him to knock it off, but I couldn't bring myself to do it. Heck, that sweet, appreciative look on his face was enough to make me want to fall into bed with him again and again. My pride be damned.

"Come on you guys!" Annie pulled us and we trotted after her dutifully.

When we reached the tiger exhibit, Christian and I took turns reading the plaques with facts about the animal.

She narrowed her eyes and screwed up her mouth.

I could only guess that she was meticulously memorizing every fact for later. She had a knack for it.

“Take a picture of us,” Christian asked me, holding out his cellphone.

"Okay, smile," I called to her and Christian as they stood in front of the exhibit.

I took a picture of them and looked at it on the phone. Annie had smiled so hard it made love well up in my heart for her and Christian actually looked happy. That stern look that he often wore always dissolved when he held his daughter.

Christian took his phone back and stopped someone walking past. "Can you take a picture of the three of us?"

I felt my face heat up. "You want me in it?" I asked.

"Of course," he said with a grin. "You're here too, right?"

“Well—”

"Come on, Hannah!" Annie shouted loudly. "You gotta take the picture with us."

I laughed and caved right away.

A woman took Christian's phone and aimed it at us as he wrapped an arm around my shoulder. Annie sat in the middle on both of our shoulders until the picture was taken.

The woman walked over and handed it to Christian. "You guys are such a cute little family. It's nice to see that these days."

I didn’t know where to look or what to say.

Christian had no such problems. "Thank you," he told her smoothly.

The woman smiled and walked off to join her friends and we

all peered at the picture. I could kind of understand why she thought we were a family. We looked amazing. The way we were all smiling at the camera, so carefree, and happy.

Annie tugged my hair lightly. "You look pretty."

"So do you," I replied instantly. "Look at that cute dimple."

"What dimple?" she asked cheekily.

I poked her cheek. "That thing on your face that makes your smile sparkle."

When I turned I found Christian staring at his screen. "Christian?"

He glanced up at me and shoved his phone into his pocket. “Yeah. Okay, let’s go to the next exhibit.” He took Annie's free hand and we headed on to go look at penguins and get lunch.

Then every time I glanced at Christian, he was staring at me. What the hell was going on?

I wanted to tell him that he was making me die from internal heat, but instead, I soldiered on. No matter how much I tried to ignore it, however, I could feel his eyes on me. I would pay good money to see what was going on inside of that head of his. I couldn’t understand why he kept blowing hot and cold.

By the time we'd finished up saying hello to all the animals, the sun was going down.

Annie looked half out of it and she dozed off inside of the car. I pulled a blanket up over her lap and made sure she was comfortable before I turned back around and sighed happily. "That was so much fun. I haven't been to the zoo in ages."

"We went last year, but it was a completely different experience..." Christian paused. "Thanks for going with us. I know how much that meant to her. And it's nice to have a second set of feet to chase her down."

"She is pretty fast. Why do all kids have such hyper drive?"

"It's built in at birth," Christian said with a grin.

We drove in silence for a while and I became very aware that his arm was very close to mine as it rested next to the console. I swear I could feel the heat radiating off of his body and I wanted him to inch over and touch me. My fingers tingled near his, but eventually he brushed over my hand as if it was nothing. I glanced at him, but he kept his eyes trained on the road.

By the time we made it to the house, Annie was awake and ready to go again. She zoomed into the house as Christian and I unpacked the goodies she'd brought back with her. As we got through the door, our bodies accidentally brushed together and I had to bite my lip from making a fool of myself.

"Stay for dinner?" Christian asked as he set the bags down in the entryway.

He was so close I could smell his cologne, his shampoo, the scent of his sun kissed skin itself.

"That's, if you want to," he added. "I know you've been around here a lot. You could probably use some time to yourself."

I shook my head and tucked away a stray hair that had come loose. "I don't know."

Christian leaned closer to me. "I have something to ask you after dinner. A little proposal. If you stick around."

I stared at his lips and couldn't rip my eyes away.

“Hey,” those lips said.

When I looked up, his green eyes captured me and held me in place.

I nodded my head. "I'll stay. Your food is kind of addictive."

"Good," he said huskily. "I'll talk to you about it after dinner." Christian broke the spell when he tore his gaze away and headed off to the kitchen.

I watched him until he disappeared. I wanted to rock that man's world.

Did you really just think that?

I ran a hand over my face. I have to find a solution to this reaction I have every time I am around him and I need to find it fast.

Chapter Seventeen

HANNAH

Dinner was a mix of heaven and *what the hell.*

I tried to ignore the tingling that raced up and down my spine, but that was impossible to do with Christian so near me. We ate, laughed and talked as if everything was normal, but every once in a while, his eyes caught mine and everything changed. The very air around us became molten with unspoken lust.

With dinner over, Annie looked exhausted. It was a short nap she had in the car and it had been an action-packed day.

I waved Christian away and told him to read her a story while I cleaned up on my own. I didn't mind doing it and I needed some time to get my head on straight.

Christian wandered back down just as I finished up. He smiled at my handiwork. "Perfect as usual," he whispered.

"Didn't you know I'm a Stepford wife?" I joked.

He leaned on the doorframe and stared at me.

I chewed at my lip. "What?" I asked. "You've been staring at me all day."

He pushed himself off of the doorframe and strolled over to me.

My heart was drumming like crazy in my chest as he walked closer and closer. He reached me and I felt like I couldn't breathe.

His hand caressed my cheek, down the side of my neck and rested on my waist. "I can't stop thinking about you," he breathed. "I want you so damn bad it's ridiculous. All I think about is you lately."

I swallowed hard. I knew exactly what he meant. "I want you too," I admitted. "I have for a while."

Christian nodded and pulled his hand away.

I longed for that warmth to come back and invade my space once more, but he seemed like he had something to say.

He pushed his fingers through his hair and looked me up and down. "We need to set some ground rules."

"Like what?" I asked.

"I don't want this to interfere with Annie in any way," he said seriously.

I shook my head. "I don't either. She comes first."

Christian nodded. "Exactly. And the other thing is that I don't do relationships. If we're going to do this, all it can be is sex. Nothing more, okay?"

"Just sex?" I asked.

"Yes. I don't have time in my life for anything serious. You have to agree that this is only a temporary thing."

It was like a punch to the gut. All he wanted was sex. I could swear at times he wanted so much more when he looked at me, but then that cold facade came back into place and I wasn't so sure anymore.

Can I really handle a no strings relationship?

I knew there was more beneath the surface than attraction when I looked at Christian. He had so many positive attributes that I appreciated in a man, and it made me want more, but I couldn't push him into doing more when that wasn't what he wanted. All I could control was myself and my decision to sleep with him or not.

What if you fall for him, a voice in my head asked.

His proposal felt like a bad idea, a very bad idea, but his eyes burned into mine with such fierce passion that my knees felt weak. If I said no, I would regret it until my dying day. Better to have loved... I was nodding before I even realized I was doing it. "Okay," I said firmly. "Just sex. Nothing else. I'm okay with that."

Christian examined my face and my expression. "Are you sure?"

I nodded. "I'm sure," I breathed. "I just want you."

Christian stepped close so fast and kissed me so hard my head started to spin. I wilted against his body, my mind shut off against the negatives for the moment. Screw everything else. I wanted him, I had to have him, and I wasn't going to deny myself something amazing even if it wasn't permanent.

He pushed me back against the counter and lifted me onto it. My legs wrapped around his waist as I parted my lips and accepted his eager tongue. He pushed it into my mouth, hooked my tongue into his mouth and sucked on it until I moaned against him. His nails scratched my scalp and every inch of my body tingled tantalizingly.

I moaned against him. "Don't hold back."

"You want me?" he asked as his hands moved underneath my shirt running down my back.

"You know I do."

"I don't care. Say it," he demanded.

"I want you," I whispered. "I want you to take me upstairs and fuck me until I can't walk. I want you to kiss me until my lips are swollen. I want you to do whatever you want to my body."

Christian growled against my mouth.

I watched the shift in him that I'd seen that first night in his car.

That distant, cold exterior melted away— he was now all fire and red-hot heat. He lifted me off the counter and tossed me over his shoulder.

"What are you doing?" I laughed as he turned and strode out of the kitchen.

"Taking you to my bedroom, obviously."

"Put me down you caveman," I said as I hit his back playfully. "You could have just asked me to walk."

"This is faster."

I trembled inside. When we made it into his bedroom, he dropped me on his big bed and I bounced before I came to a stop.

Christian disappeared out of the room and came back a minute later throwing the lock on his door. "The coast is clear."

"Every time I'm with you it feels like I'm back to my days of sneaking around as a teenager," I said as I rested on my elbows.

"That's because children are tiny parents and no one can tell me otherwise." Christian got on the bed and climbed on top of me.

As soon as his body covered mine, I melted all over again. How did I always manage to go from happy, relaxed, to a turned on hot mess with him?

His hands gripped my shirt and he yanked it over my head. He tossed it to the side and came back for more. My bra ended up with my shirt. "Jesus Hannah," he exclaimed, staring greedily at my naked breasts.

I sank my teeth into my bottom lip shyly. It felt good to be appreciated by him.

He cupped my tits by the sides and buried his face into my ample flesh. His tongue traced over each nipple before he captured one in his mouth and sucked.

My head pushed back into his pillow and I cried out quietly. I reminded myself there was a child in the house and I had to be quiet. I tossed my palm over my mouth and forced myself to be quiet even if it was the hardest thing I'd ever had to do!

Heck, my boss, Christian West was sucking on my nipples and flicking his tongue over them. Had the world gone mad? Had I gone mad?

He pressed me back into the mattress with his body.

I could feel the shape of his cock as it pressed against me. Christian pushed his body against mine and I wanted to desperately rip his pants off and feel him pressed inside of me. "Shit," I whispered. "Come on."

"Not yet," he mumbled with my nipple still in his teeth.

I groaned as he licked down my breasts. Goosebumps pimpled my flesh as the air hit it. He slid his hard body down lower. His fingers slid the rest of my clothes off and his hands ran down my thighs. He pushed them up before he licked the inside of one.

I shivered. "You're kind of an asshole," I breathed.

Christian chuckled and nipped my thigh. "Why do you say that?"

"You really love to push my buttons," I countered unsteadily.

He groaned against my skin.

I fought off another of those damned shivers. His tongue dragged and swirled over my skin making it wet and sensitive. I was enraptured with the fire that lurked in his eyes.

"I love to push this button," he mumbled as he palmed my clit.

I gasped.

"You like it too, apparently."

"Apparently," I choked out as my head dipped back and I stopped fighting him. He could torture me for the rest of the night and I would be completely and hopelessly up for it. A thick finger explored my slit before he plunged it inside me and crooked it toward him. Bliss shot through my blood and boiled it until my fingers clung to his shoulders. "Come on," I panted. "Fuck me."

"Not yet. Not until you're begging for it," he growled and worked his finger in deeper before he added another and rubbed against my spot.

My legs trembled in his big capable hands as he manipulated my body like a conductor in front of his orchestra. The result was a symphony of stuttered moans, tight gasps, and a high squeaky version of my voice as I begged him to take me. I wasn't ashamed of it. I wanted him so badly I could feel the want in my bones.

The symphony reached a crescendo as my back arched and I came so hard I couldn't breathe. I screamed out my pleasure. Thank God, he crushed my mouth with his to muffle the sound.

The waves of pleasure receded and I fell limp against the pillow.

Christian stood up.

My weary, glazed eyes examined him closely. I watched as he tugged off his clothes and tossed them to the side revealing a hard body that begged to be touched. My tongue came out to lick my bottom lip as his pants and boxers disappeared to reveal an enormous hard, throbbing cock.

It stood up and slid along his stomach under the low lights in his room. I could see the pre-cum beaded on the head of that beautiful dick making it look sleek and shiny. My mouth watered at the thought of tasting him. Before I even knew I wanted to move, I was already on my knees in front of him. I fisted the impressive length, squeezed, and stroked it as I took in the heady scent of his manhood.

"Fuck," he groaned hoarsely. "Do you have to worship it like that?"

"It's a beautiful thing," I whispered as I gazed up at him. "And it's like this just for me."

Christian's breath caught in his throat and he stared at me almost in disbelief.

I leaned forward and flicked my tongue over his sensitive flesh.

He hissed lightly and his face contorted as I dragged my tongue against his slit to collect his sticky, salty juices, just like a child would a piece of candy. My fingers caressed and fondled his balls before I slid him into my mouth completely.

The tight, hotness of my throat enclosed around him, and he damn near pitched forward. His hands gripped my hair, fisting it, as he rocked his hips forward intently. Saliva dripped down my chin and the curve of my throat as he positioned his cock forward, eager for more pleasure. I twisted my head and stroked him with my tongue. Slowly, deliberately I sucked and stroked him.

Suddenly, he yanked himself free and growled with his hand gripped tightly at the base of his cock. "Get on the fucking bed."

Christian didn't have to tell me twice. I climbed in and he

was on me in a second. Our mouths crashed together, our tongues fighting for dominance as he rocked and rolled his hard cock against my belly.

I gasped, my fingers grabbing his flesh before I panted against his mouth. "If you don't fuck me right now I'll fuck myself and leave you with blue balls."

“Do that and I’ll tan your hide so good you won’t sit for a week,” he threatened.

“Do it if you dare,” I challenged.

Something flashed in his eyes. “All in good time. Your ass will be red one of these days.”

I grinned with anticipation and he kissed me once more before leaning over to the bedside table. When he came back up, he had a condom packet in his hand. As he ripped it open, he said. “Open your legs wide and play with your pussy.”

While my fingers obeyed his command, I watched him roll the rubber on with agonizing slowness.

Languidly, his lips met mine and I moaned against him. I felt the head of his thick cock as it grazed my slit. Slowly, he pushed it inside of me. Each inch was a gloriously painful pleasure as I adjusted and stretched to accommodate him. He took his time and rocked his hips slowly as he pushed in bit by slow bit.

“Oh, God,” I gasped.

By the time he bottomed out, my breasts heaved and pushed against his body.

He licked his lips and stared down at me, his eyes were sparking with lust and desire.

My eyes fluttered in surprise as his hand caressed my cheek and he kissed me softly. I melted against that softness and craved more, but just like that, it was gone.

Christian then thrust inside of me hard, rough and strong.

I cried out and wrapped my arms around him as he gripped my hips and rocked himself deeper. My toes curled as the slapping sounds of our bodies meeting echoed through the room. Wet skin against skin, the smell of our sex and the taste of sweat on our lips only turned me on more.

He took his time and slipped between hard, fast and frenzied, to slow and teasing. Each thrust pushed me closer and closer to the edge as I surrendered to the bliss I felt. Christian's tongue traced my throat and I groaned as I pushed up into him and clenched my pussy around his hard cock.

"Fuck," he swore sharply. "Don't do that."

"This?" I purred, repeating the movement.

“Yes,” he confirmed with a strangled sound.

I clenched down again and he grunted against me. He pushed himself up, grabbed my thighs and pushed them up until my ankles were damn well near my ears. I cried out and swiftly slapped a hand over my mouth as he pumped in and out of me in that position. He slammed deeper and banged against my G spot with a scary, ferocious accuracy that sent me hurtling toward the edge of my abyss.

"I have to come," I groaned as I shoved my hand between my thighs and worked my already oversensitive clit. "Harder. Don't hold back."

Christian grunted in response. I knew, like me, he too was too far gone to form a proper sentence. Instead, his pace increased to a point of almost madness. His breathing deepened as he rammed his throbbing cock into me. Again and again.

I threw my head back as the orgasm that had built in my belly released hard. Tingling from head to toe I writhed and convulsed as it swept over me and drowned me. Moments later, I felt Christian thrust hard and deep one last time before he too found his release. Then he pulled free and collapsed next to me.

We didn't say a word as we tried to collect ourselves. I watched as sweat pooled and ran down his exquisite body. My heart ached a little in my chest, but a deal was a deal. I knew I had to remember the truth of it.

This was just sex. Nothing more.

Chapter Eighteen

HANNAH

"You're late." Natalie grinned as I hustled into the coffee shop.

"Sorry," I mumbled. "I'm all over the place this morning. Let me get my drink."

Natalie waved a hand. "Here, I already got it for you. Cappuccino, extra whip."

I groaned happily, as I took the cup and settled myself opposite her. My body protested, still sore from my night with Christian. We hadn't stopped after the first time as if we had to keep going at each other to get any kind of satisfaction. "I didn't make it home until this morning."

Natalie raised a brow. "This morning? What happened?"

I fidgeted with my cup and took a sip that burned my tongue.

She rolled her eyes. "Really? You'd rather burn your mouth than tell me?"

I shrugged. "A little."

"What did you do Hannah?"

I sighed. "All right. I slept with Christian."

"What!" she shouted dramatically.

I slid down in my seat a bit, as the gazes of other customers flew in our direction. My cheeks flushed underneath those stares and I glared at her warningly. Once people turned back to their coffee and computers, I sat forward. "For God's sake, Natalie," I hissed.

"I'm sorry, you just want me to what? Ignore the fact that you're fucking your super-hot boss?"

I dropped my head into my palm. "It's just a casual thing. We ended up in bed together and that's the end of that."

"It's definitely not. What do you mean casual? I've never known you to do a casual thing in your life. You're either full on, or not at all."

I shrugged. "It's what he wants."

"What he wants?" she yelled, her face becoming red with fury.

"But I agreed to it. He didn't force me or anything. He just doesn't do relationships. So, it's going to have to be a casual thing or nothing."

"And that's okay with you."

"Not completely, but if I had said no, I would have regretted it all my life. I would have wondered what it would have been like." I crinkled my nose. "Although, I do get a little worried that I might end up falling for him. The last thing I need is a heartbreak."

"Exactly," Natalie said evenly. "Which is why I think you must have bumped your head and gone insane to agree to something like that."

"Maybe," I muttered as I toyed with my straw. "He's just unlike any guy I've ever met. He's so sexy and dominant, but he can be sweet and gentle too. When he laughs, it makes my whole body tingle. And you should see him with Annie. The two of them together is enough to melt anyone's heart."

"That's what worries me," Natalie said softly. "Listen to how you're talking about him already. You've put him on a pedestal and all the guy wants to do is fuck you."

"Natalie..."

She waved a hand. "I'm not saying you can't fuck him. I'm not even saying it's a bad thing to want to climb into his bed. You're both adults and that makes it all okay, but the problem is you're the type of person to get your heart involved. In everything. What if this all goes bad and you can't see him again? What if you can't see his daughter? Can you honestly say that you'd be okay after a blow like that?"

I gritted my teeth. "Despite what everyone seems to think, I'm a big girl, Nat. I know how to handle myself, and even if I get hurt... so be it. It's part of life. I'll survive the way everybody else does when their heart gets broken."

She sipped her coffee. "Okay, no need to get snippy with me. I just want what's best for you. Did he say why he wanted things to stay casual?"

I shrugged. "Maybe he's been hurt before or maybe he just

doesn't have time for a full-blown relationship. He's off running his company most of the time."

"Or are those all excuses that you're telling yourself?"

I chewed my bottom lip. I should have known that Natalie would cut me to the quick. She wasn't the type to mince her words. On the other hand, I knew there wasn't any ill-intent behind her words. She really did just want what was best for me, what would make me happy. I could see the concern on her face as she gazed at me and I had to give it to her. She had some valid points.

Still, I wanted Christian.

Every time I thought about his sexy smile, his easy-going laugh, and the way he loved his daughter I was putty in his hands all over again. It was easy not to love someone who was a jerk, but Christian wasn't that. Even if he didn't want anything serious, he was still considerate and kind and he was honest about what he wanted. He didn't string me along.

Before I'd left this morning, he'd woken me up early like I'd asked. I still remembered the kiss he'd pressed to my shoulder followed by the nip when I wouldn't wake up. His mischievous grin had made every part of my body heat up and we'd had another sex session again before the sun was even up. I wanted more moments like that. Maybe I couldn't have him forever, but I could have him for a while.

I knew not everything was meant to last forever.

But even now that thought was already making my stomach twist even though I knew as well as he did that we would never work out. We were from two completely different worlds. But maybe Natalie was wrong. I could have some fun with a hot guy that made me orgasm a million times in a row and still do my job, and be happy once I had convinced myself anything else was out of reach.

"I'll be okay," I said and smiled at her. "I know you're worried, but it will all come out in the wash and I'll be the wiser for it. You'll see."

"For your sake? I sure hope so. Just be careful, okay? Guys like him are hard to replace. Are you prepared for that?"

"I don't know," I answered honestly. "What I do know is that I want to stick things out with him and see where it goes."

Natalie looked me over before she nodded. "Fair enough," she said as she stirred her coffee. "So, how big is his dick?"

"Nat!" I scolded.

Two middle-aged women at the table next to us looked scandalized.

She grinned so hard I thought her face would crack.

"You're such a bitch," I whispered, shaking my head at her.

"Well?" she prodded.

"Enormous," I said with a small squeal.

We both laughed.

Chapter Nineteen

HANNAH

"What do you want to watch?" I asked Annie.

"Hmm, I don't know."

"You've vetoed all of my choices," I said with an exaggerated sigh.

"What's a veto?"

"That means you said no. Annie, please pick a movie. My heart just can't take the rejection anymore." I clutched my shirt dramatically.

She giggled at my antics then bounded across the room, snatched the remote out of my hand and plopped onto the couch. We'd spent our morning playing dress up in the back-yard after breakfast. It turned into afternoon swim time and then lunch. Now I was exhausted, and just looking forward to sitting down and just watching something.

"Can we watch Moana?" Annie asked.

I narrowed my eyes. "Isn't that the first thing I suggested?"

Annie gave me a sheepish grin.

I threw a pillow at her and she giggled as we took turns flinging it at each other before I called an end to hostilities then left the media room. I went to the kitchen and popped a bag popcorn. The perfect snack to go with our movie.

We settled in on the big leather couch and palmed popcorn by the handful into our mouths. Manners had gone out of the window for the sake of screaming and yelling lyrics laughing. We finished the first movie and Annie quickly found another one.

I checked the time.

"Daddy's late." She sighed.

"Yes, but he should be here soon. I'm sure he's working hard."

"Should we do something nice for him soon? If he's working hard, I don't want him to get too tired," she said seriously.

"That would be sweet," I said. "Why don't we make him a lunch tomorrow and surprise him? We'll steal him and have a picnic."

Annie's eyes lit up. "Can we keep it a secret?"

"Of course. Surprises are supposed to be secret." I chuckled.

"Oooo... I can't wait."

I watched her bounce happily, as she settled in for another movie. We cuddled up underneath a blanket together and before I knew it, my eyes grew heavy. I glanced over at Annie.

Her eyelids were drooping and her head nodded forward before she shot it back up and tried to focus on the TV. That didn't last for more than a minute before her eyes closed again. She was the cutest thing ever.

I must have dozed off because when I came to, the media room was lit by the TV screen and my pussy was soaking wet. I jolted and glanced down. Christian had knelt in front of me still in his suit and tie from work. My skirt was pushed up my thighs and because I wasn't wearing panties on his orders, he was happily licking at my wetness.

My eyes darted around the room, but Annie was nowhere to be found.

He looked up. My juices were smeared on his reddened lips, making them look glossy in the low light. "I took Annie to her bed and tucked her in. We have some time to ourselves now," he breathed in that husky voice of his.

His sensual tone shook me to my core. "And this is how you wake a girl up?" I asked.

"Complaints?"

I didn't have a single one. Languidly, I settled back to enjoy being eaten out.

Christian pushed my legs even further apart and went right back to lapping at my slit. He shoved his tongue inside of me.

I felt it swipe at my walls and clenched around it, grinding my hips against his face as he rubbed and stroked my swollen clit. "Christian..." I gasped.

He pulled his tongue free and lapped at my clit. "Shhh. Just sit back and relax."

I stared down at him as his tongue swirled and lapped all over my sex.

He collected every drop of wetness he could as if he couldn't get enough of my flavor. He gazed up at me and pushed his fingers into my pussy. "You're so hot," he mumbled as our eyes locked. "Every bit of you is hot."

I bit my lip and took in a shuddering breath. The double entendre wasn't lost on me as I slid down further and let my legs fall completely open for him. He pulled his fingers free from me and reached his hand up. As I licked his fingers and tasted myself on his skin, I watched as he reached down and undid his slacks. He opened them, pushed them down his toned thighs and worked his hand over his already straining cock.

I gripped his wrist and swirled my tongue around his fingers slowly. I sucked them in deep, lapped between each one, and twisted my head before I pulled them free.

Christian watched, mesmerized until he came back to life, and shivered. "You're way too fucking good at that."

"At what?" I purred as I licked his finger. "All I'm doing is cleaning up the dirty, dirty mess you made."

"Hell, I'm about to make another one."

I grinned wickedly. It was such a thrill having control over a man like Christian. The way his eyes went all starry and lust-filled made me feel like a queen. He stroked his cock harder and I watched as a pearly drop appeared at his slit before it flowed over and coated his hand.

"You make me so wet," I moaned.

He leaned forward and attacked my pussy again. A strangled grunt left his lips at my words and he picked up speed.

I felt the orgasm that approached and tried to push his head away from me. I wanted to make it last. I was having too much fun.

Christian was having none of it. He grabbed my hand and shoved it away as he lapped at my pussy furiously.

"Christian," I panted. "Wait."

Of course, he ignored me and kept up his attentions. I twined my fingers into his hair, arched my back, and cried out. It was too much. I rode his face as I came hard, my moans caught in my throat as I shivered and trembled in his hands.

Christian came up for air and grinned. He looked like a wild beast that wanted to devour me. I'd probably let him. Hey, it was a good way to go.

He looked proud of himself as he settled down on the couch next to me. He leaned back, his palm stroking his cock as he gazed at me. When he reached over, it was to tease and tug on my nipples. To my surprise, my exhaustion had completely worn off and my fire was lit once again.

I moved from the couch and climbed on top of him. My hands ripped at his shirt. The buttons flew across the room as his chest was exposed to me. I traced my fingers over his abs, over his nipples and down his sides. I couldn't get enough of touching him. "Was that a very expensive shirt?" I purred.

“Why? Do you want to make it up to me?”

I fluttered my eyelashes hard enough to do Jessica Rabbit proud. "I'm sorry. How should I make it up to you?"

"I can think of several things." He gripped my ass before his hand slapped against my skin.

I quivered and pushed back against it wanting more as I dug my hand into the pockets of his slacks. His wallet tumbled into my hands and I yanked it open. I smiled when I saw the foil lined condom. "Always prepared, aren't you?"

"You're always around. How could I not be?"

His words made my heart speed up. The fact that he was so turned on by me was amazing and I loved the fact that he constantly wanted me. I put the condom between my teeth before I slipped down his body and settled myself onto my knees.

I ripped open the condom and held it in my fingertips as I lapped at the angry red head of his cock. It constantly leaking, dripping, and ready to be licked by my tongue. Every time the taste of his saltiness touched in my tongue, it gave me a high quite unlike any I've known. I placed the condom over his heavy cock and wrapped my lips around the head and latex.

I pushed down and the condom unfurled itself around his hard shaft. It gripped him snugly. Slowly I lowered my head. Inch after inch he sank into my lips until my lips were pressed against his groin. He was nestled in my throat, throbbing and rock hard as I gazed up at him with a victorious look.

"Hannah," he groaned. "Fuck, you're too much you know that?"

I could only hum in agreement. That vibration sent his hips jerking as he bucked into my throat. I came up for air as I wiped saliva from my lips and chin as he watched with admiration. He scrambled to get up, but I pushed against his chest and straddled his lap.

"Do you want me to fuck you?" I whispered.

Christian nodded hard. "So damn bad."

I didn't tease him, I wasn't that cruel. Instead, I gripped his cock and steadied it before I slowly let myself sink down on his hard flesh. He bucked, jolted, moaned, and grunted as I took him in. By the time he'd bottomed out inside of me, I was in heaven.

"Too much?" he asked with a smug grin on his lips.

My answer was to lift myself upwards and slam back down hard.

My nipples were peaked hard as pleasure swept through me. Suddenly, I was lost. I raised and lowered myself again and again as the sound of my wet pussy hitting his groin reached my ears.

Christian was a wild man. He spanked my ass until it felt as if my cheeks were glowing. I shoved a hand between us and stroked my clit until the point of ecstasy. When I became too tired to bounce on his cock, Christian had no problem moving me. He grabbed my hips and guided me up and down as I moaned and held on for dear life.

Our mouths connected and our tongues caressed each other. We kissed so hard our teeth clashed, but we didn't care. Together, we panted and moaned.

Then he held me in place and began to ram into me. After that first rough thrust, he rutted like he was desperate for my pussy until he bucked and swore. "Need to come," he groaned. "Right now."

I wrapped my legs around his back. "Come for me baby."

Christian gripped me hard, his breath in my ear as he worked himself harder.

His cock twitched and pulsed inside me as I clenched down and buried my face in the crook of his neck. At that moment, a powerful orgasm tore through me and left me spent. I was high among the clouds, with him buried deep inside me, as he found his release.

We stayed wrapped up in each other's arms for a long time. Neither of us wanting to move. The heat and closeness of his body lulled me into a comfortable state. I yawned and nestled against him.

He gazed down at me.

"What?" I asked quietly.

Christian shook his head.

I wanted to ask what he was thinking about, but I knew it was better to leave it alone at the moment.

I was content.

He was content.

There was no reason to ruin the moment.

Chapter Twenty

CHRISTIAN

"What the hell are you doing?" I asked as I stepped through the door and stared.

"We were—um—it's a long story," Hannah said sheepishly.

"Why are you both covered in paint?"

"We're paintings Daddy, duh!"

"Yeah, duh." Hannah grinned. "Clearly, we belong somewhere hung up in museums."

Both of them were painted head to toe in a barrage of colorful pastels. Annie had whiskers on her face. Hannah sported hearts and shapes on her cheeks. I could see the paint as it extended up and down their bodies, both of them covered as they stood there in their swimsuits. My eyes softened at Annie, but when they landed on Hannah—it was a different story.

Damn, she looked amazing.

I had a harder time denying my intense attraction, or her with each passing day. It had been a little over a week since we'd started having sleepovers. As she stood there in the bright blue bikini, brown hair trailing down her shoulders and those deep blue eyes trained on me, I felt my heart skip a beat. There was no way any woman should look so beautiful when covered in paint. It struck me then that unlike all my past relationships, I still wasn't bored with our arrangement. I loved it. I loved having her.

I wagged a finger at both of them. "Don't you two start. And don't say duh. Is Hannah teaching you bad habits?"

Annie smiled. "No, Daddy. Hannah is the bestest nanny ever."

"See?" Hannah huffed. "The bestest. How dare you?"

I sighed and shook my head. The two of them together were a force to be reckoned with and I often found myself outvoted. So far, we'd gone mini golfing, played at an in-the-dark-glow tag place, gone fishing and visited the waterpark. Twice. They both loved to rip and run. I felt like the old man trying to keep up.

"Go upstairs and pick out your clothes for after your bath," I told Annie. "How are we going to eat dinner if you're covered in paint?"

"Like this," she said as she mimicked eating with the very tips of her fingers and teeth.

"Go," I said as she giggled and ran off. When she was up the stairs, I stalked closer to Hannah. "What am I going to do with you?"

"I thought we already discussed hanging me in a museum." She grinned. "I am a work of art, after all."

"You're a piece of work," I grumbled. "Don't know about art."

Hannah flourished her brush and poked it into my cheek. When I gasped at her, the grin only widened and she quickly started to pack up her paints.

I grabbed her and yanked her against my body.

Her eyes went wide when she felt my erection. "Annie will be back down. What are you doing?"

"Can those paints be used upstairs?" I asked.

Hannah chuckled. "Not really, but I did also buy the edible kind," she breathed.

My dick jumped to attention immediately. I hated when she used that husky, breathy voice to fuck with my head. It always worked and I was left wanting and waiting until bedtime rolled around.

As if she'd read my mind, she reached down, gripped my cock and squeezed through my slacks.

"That is just uncalled for," I scolded. "You don't play fair."

"Who ever said I was fair?" She clicked her tongue. "That seems more like your problem than mine."

I shuddered as she rubbed me through my pants. The warmth of her hand against my hardness made me want to turn her around and fuck her against the counter. I gripped her hair and kissed her hard until we were both breathless and panting in each other's arms. "Don't tease me," I warned. "You know how good I am at punishing you."

"Maybe I want to be punished," she purred against my lips. "You don't know what I'm into." Hannah grinned at me.

I felt myself grow harder. *How the hell can one woman drive me so insane? She was damn good at it too.*

"Daddy! I'm ready for my bath now," Annie sang from the top of the stairs.

"I'm coming honey," I called up before I gripped the back of Hannah's neck and pulled her close. I planted one more kiss on her plump lips before I quickly turned and walked away. I was going to get myself into trouble. And I welcomed it.

After bath time for Annie and a shower for Hannah, both of them were clean again. They both had faintly pink skin. Hannah smelled like the citrus body wash that she'd smuggled into my shower. She didn't like smelling like pine apparently. But she liked it when it was on my skin. One lick of me made her writhe with passion and bliss.

Hannah was kind of perfect.

We had our dinner in front of the TV for once. The sound of the cartoon played through as I glanced over at Hannah. She caught my eye and smiled before she licked her bottom lip then, let her teeth sink into the plumpness.

I swallowed hard.

Damn it.

She knew just how to keep me hanging on. As soon as dinner was finished, I tucked Annie in and came back downstairs to help with the dishes. I found her with her headphones on her ears while singing and rocking her hips. I froze, mesmerized by her. Hannah was effortlessly beautiful. It tightened something in my chest and made me crave her. As I watched, she wiped a hand across her cheek.

I walked up to her, wrapped my arms around her waist and kissed her throat.

She jumped and hit me with soapy hands. "Don't just sneak up on someone," she scolded.

"Why not? I never saw you dancing before, or heard you singing like that."

Hannah grinned. "There's a lot about me you don't know."

Those words bothered me for some reason. I knew what we were doing was just sex, but she was right. There was so much about her that I didn't know. I wanted to find out more. I kissed her nose.

She smiled.

"I wanted to talk to you about something," I said seriously, stepping back and releasing her.

She frowned. "What is it?"

"Nothing to worry about," I said quickly to relieve her fears. "I actually wanted to talk to you about how much you've been staying over lately. I figured if you're going to be spending the night so much over here, you might as well move in."

Hannah blinked at me. "What?”

“I figured if you're going to be spending the night so much over here you might as well move in,” I repeated.

“Are you asking me to move in?" she asked incredulously.

I laughed. "What else would you think I'm saying?"

She slapped my arm. "Don't be a jerk. I'm just surprised."

"Well, what do you say?" I asked as I wrapped my arms back around her. "Annie loves you, and I would love it if you were here full time."

Hannah tapped a finger against her chin. "I'm not so sure about that. Let me think it over."

I blinked at her in surprise.

She burst out laughing.

I groaned and rolled my eyes. Of course, she was screwing with me. I grabbed her and hugged her.

"Of course, I'll stay. I love working here and I like you too. It'll be nice not to have to commute so much."

I sighed in relief. "Next time, don't give me a heart attack."

"I'll try to behave," she purred.

"I highly doubt that," I mumbled as my lips hovered over hers.

We kissed and she sighed against me. My body grew hot just at that sound. I was on dangerous ground. I knew that. With Hannah, I had to be careful or things might unravel in a bad way.

Chapter Twenty-One

HANNAH

I'd settled into the house nicely and without too much fuss. Christian had helped me with the few boxes I brought, and Annie with decorating my room. My usually downplayed colors had taken on a noticeably pink theme in my bedroom, but she liked it better that way. Every morning when I walked out of my room, Annie threw her arms around me and told me how happy she was that I was living with them.

At first, I'd been apprehensive about the move.

Sleeping with Christian was one thing, living with him was entirely something else. I knew there was a real possibility that I might fall for him and I knew that wasn't what he wanted.

It wasn't what I want either. I kept trying to convince myself that was true, but it was hard. How could anyone not fall for Christian? He was funny, strong, sexy, and a complete sweetheart. Just thinking about him made me smile. I quickly wiped it off of my face and glanced up as loud knocking came from my door. "Gee, I wonder who that could be?"

A giggle came from the other side. "It's Annie."

“Oh, right.”

“Are you going to read me a story?" she asked from outside.

I opened my door and smiled at her. "I thought Daddy was reading it to you."

"He was, but I want you to come tonight." She grabbed my hand. "Come on. Daddy reads one and then you read one."

"Ah, is that how it works?"

She nodded vigorously. "Yep!"

I shook my head and smiled at her softly. Ever since I'd moved in, she hadn't wanted to be away from me. The other night she'd had a sleepover in my room and we'd stayed up watching movies, painting our nails, and trying to hunt Christian down for a makeover. He'd avoided us just in time.

“Let’s go then,” I said and we walked to her bedroom together.

Christian glanced up and grinned at me. He was still dressed in his work clothes minus the jacket, and looked pretty edible. I wanted to fan myself as I settled in. I was given my reading assignment for the night and we both read our allotted books until Annie passed out while clutching one of her bears.

"My room?" Christian asked.

"God, yes. I've been waiting all day."

Christian laughed. "Somebody has no shame."

"Shame? I want to fuck you. What's so shameful about that?"

“If you have to ask then there is no hope for you.”

I winked seductively at him which made him laugh.

We were so desperate for each other that we didn’t even make it to the bed. I got fucked standing and pushed up against the door. By the time he'd finished, I was hot and exhausted. He carried me to bed and I curled up against him. He wrapped an arm around me while I tried to catch my breath.

"I was just thinking that you keep surprising me. Honestly, it's like when I think I know everything about you then I realize I don't know a thing. You intrigue the hell out of me," he whispered in my hair.

I smiled. "I'm nothing but myself. That's it."

"It's more than that," Christian said with a shake of his head. "You're really fascinating."

I could feel my cheeks start to burn. I wasn't used to compliments being showered on me so generously. Not knowing what to say, I traced a finger over his abs and enjoyed the smoothness of his skin. "Can I ask you something?”

“Ask away,” he said lazily.

“Why is it you don't do relationships?”

He froze.

Now, I wished I had never asked as a weird silence filled the room.

Then he started speaking, "My ex-wife cheated on me with my half-brother." He laughed dryly. "My brother has always hated me and constantly wanted to get back at me because I'm my father's favorite. It's not like I can help that or even agree with my father showing favoritism, but now he's bitter about the whole thing. Anyway, Daphne up and left me and Annie for him. I thought we had something permanent and she just walked away from everything like we were both nothing. People warned me, in the beginning, she was only chasing the money, but I didn't listen."

"I'm so sorry," I whispered. "That sounds awful."

Christian shrugged. "It's in the past, but it has given me trust issues. I look at everyone twice and question their motives. I promised myself that I would never leave myself that vulnerable again in a relationship. I couldn't even trust my own brother. I gave him his start in life, I bought him his house, and he betrayed me. I can never forgive him."

My heart ached for him. I could hear the emotion he tried so hard to restrain, but the way his heart sped up underneath my ear showed he wasn't doing too well on that front. I wanted to take all of that pain away from him, but I knew Christian had to move past those things himself. I couldn't swoop in and save him. That's not how it worked.

I glanced up at him. "Do you think you're capable of love one day?"

Christian seemed to contemplate my words, but something on his face sent a sharp pain to my stomach. I could see the answer in his eyes before he even said a word.

Slowly, he shook his head. "No," he stated quietly. "I don't think I'll ever love again."

Just like that, the sharp twinge became a stabbing pain. Suddenly, it was hard to breathe. *Why was I doing this? Natalie was right. I'd been setting myself up for a big fall.* I'd known from the beginning that it wouldn't be more, but hearing him say he could never love me still rocked me to my core.

I nodded slowly, the only acknowledgment that I could give because if I opened my mouth, I knew I'd cry. Then I slipped out of bed and back into my clothes. The whole time I felt his eyes on me and felt the words on his lips that he never said until I put my hand on the doorknob.

"Hannah. Are we okay? I mean, we said what this was from the beginning, right?"

I glanced back at him.

Our post sex glow still clung to his body, as he looked warm and gorgeous wrapped up in his sheets.

Usually, I stayed until the very minute before I started falling asleep, but if I had to stare at that pillow tossed hair and those lips slightly puffy from kissing me I was going to lose it. "Yeah, we're okay," I answered without knowing if we really were. "I'm about to pass out though, so I'm going to bed."

"Is that the truth?" he prodded as I tried to slip away.

I wanted to tell him that hell no... that wasn't the truth. Before I'd moved in, I knew I'd fall for him, and it looked as if I'd done just that. I adored Christian. I wanted to be more than his before bedtime snack for the rest of my time in his employment. But I didn't say it. I knew it would only make him turn tail and run.

I just smiled sadly. "Of course. Don't forget to text me from work tomorrow to let me know what you'd like for dinner. Annie and I are cooking. Night, night."

Christian nodded. "Goodnight, Hannah."

I couldn't get out of the room fast enough. My feet carried me into my bedroom and I collapsed on my bed in a heap. My chest ached, my eyes burned, and I buried my face in my pillow to muffle the groan that echoed from my throat.

Natalie's words played on a loop in my brain.

How could I be so naive? There was no way I would ever be anything more to Christian than a good lay. Seriously, had I lost my mind? I curled up, yanked my blanket over my body as I squeezed my eyes tightly shut and forced myself to go to sleep.

Chapter Twenty-Two

HANNAH

I spent the entire next day questioning everything.

Christian's words replayed for me, the finality in his voice like a hammer driving it all home. I couldn't concentrate all day, half-heartedly coloring and playing with Annie until it was time for dinner. When Christian came in, I avoided his eyes and went on as if everything was normal. What choice did I have?

"How was your day?" Christian asked.

"Good. We made pictures and took out the dolls again. There was talk of the pool, but in the end, I don't think either of us was up to that. Annie's washing up for dinner."

Christian loosened his tie. "Maybe I should do the same. I'm ready to get out of this suit."

"Go ahead, you have some time. I'm finishing everything up now."

It was quiet for a second before Christian sighed. "Hannah, did I upset you last night?"

I glanced up at him and saw the anxiety on his face. I immediately felt sad for him. He didn't do anything wrong. He was honest from day one. It was me who was stupid enough to enter into this deal without thinking it through. I smiled tightly. "No, not at all. I'm fine. It's been a long day. After dinner, I'll be turning in early so you'll have to do Annie's stories."

"Okay," he said before he turned on his heels and went out.

I sighed and got back to stirring the potatoes. I know he felt confused, but I was allowed to take some time to figure things out. There would be no point in dumping all of my emotions in his lap.

Both of them came back down and sat at the table.

I sat the plates down and decided to stop sulking. Whatever happened with me and Christian I didn't want it to affect everything else. I wanted to enjoy my day. "Annie, is it good?" I asked.

She nodded. "Really, really good, but it would be better with some ketchup."

"Um... how about if you have ketchup tomorrow with your chips?"

"Yes. Will you cook that tomorrow?"

I smiled. "Of course."

"It's my turn to cook tomorrow," Christian cut in.

"I want Hannah's food."

Christian raised his eyebrows.

Annie didn't look bothered at all by the fact she'd just insulted her father.

Christian's pouting was almost cute and I could feel my heart melting all over again. I reminded myself to stop thinking about him and quickly went back to eating.

The doorbell rang in the midst of us eating.

Christian frowned. "Who the hell is that?" he muttered as he pushed his chair back and walked towards the entrance.

I'd noticed with Christian, his home was his sanctuary. He didn't have a ton of people over. Instead, if he needed to have a meeting or see some friends, he went out to a bar, or restaurant. The house itself seemed like a safe haven, a castle fortress against the rest of the world.

"Annie. Come say hi to Mommy."

I glanced up and frowned before I could stop myself.

The woman who stood there was beautiful, tall, thin, and dressed in an impeccable black dress with a long slit up on thigh. Her red hair fell around her shoulders in thick waves and her makeup looked perfect.

Daphne.

Ever since he'd said her name, I'd wondered what his ex-wife looked like. She was a bombshell. Compared to her, I felt horribly frumpy. Her icy gray eyes ran over me and dismissed me in one second flat. I gritted my teeth and glanced away before I said something I'd regret.

Christian came in after her.

Annie still hadn't moved from her spot.

"Come on, Annie. You don't want to give Mommy a hug?"

Annie curled her hand around my arm and leaned her head on me. She'd gone back to being the silent Annie that I had meet when I'd first started working for Christian.

Daphne rolled her eyes and sighed. "Always with the theatrics," she said, as she shook her head and shot me another disapproving look. "Christian, I need to speak to you. Alone."

"I'm sure you do," I mumbled under my breath before I could catch myself. My gaze shot towards Christian.

A grin tugged at the corners of his lips. He turned the grin into a cough when she turned and stared at him.

I didn't want to be petty, but something about her brought it out of me. Probably the way she talked to Annie. If she had only given me such hostile looks and used that condescending tone with just me then I would have ignored her. The way she spoke to Annie however, made my blood boil. Clearly, Annie wasn't comfortable with her.

"Christian, privately, please," Daphne said furiously.

"Whatever you have to say to me you can say in front of Hannah."

The woman gave a constipated smile. "I don't think so. This is between the two of us."

"Why don't I take Annie upstairs and get her ready for bed?" I cut in. "Dinner is just about done anyway and we have a long day tomorrow."

Christian frowned. "Are you sure?"

I waved a hand. "Of course."

Annie held out her hands to me like a baby, which kind of surprised me. I scooped her up and plopped her onto my hip. She wrapped her little arms around my throat and damn near choked me. I patted her back reassuringly. "Give Daddy goodnight kisses."

Annie leaned over and kissed him quickly.

Daphne puckered her lips. "What about your Mommy? Are you going to give her a kiss?"

Annie shook her head then buried her face into the crook of my neck.

I ran a hand down her back and turned to carry her upstairs. *Why is a part of me jealous?* I didn't want to dwell on it. Instead, I focused on Annie and tried to comfort the now almost tearful child. As I closed the door, I could hear Christian say, "Come on, Daphne. Say what you have to say."

Chapter Twenty-Three

CHRISTIAN

I watched Hannah carry my daughter upstairs. The fact that Annie wouldn't even kiss Daphne spoke volumes about their relationship. Daphne was no mother to my child. She hardly saw her, didn't pay her much attention when she did, Annie treated her worse than a stranger because of it.

When they were gone, Daphne frowned. "I don't appreciate you turning my child against me," she huffed.

I looked at her like she was stupid. "Turn her against you? I never say a bad word about you to Annie. She's a smart girl who's drawn her own conclusions and knows what you're about."

Daphne crossed her arms over her silicone chest. "What I'm about? What is that supposed to mean?"

"When was the last time you saw her?"

"Easter!" She scoffed. "You know that."

"You mean you showed up for five minutes, was annoyed with a house full of children and left after feigning a headache. She hardly even saw you."

"I did have a headache." She pouted. "All that noise didn't help. Stop being so hard on me."

I pinched the bridge of my nose. I knew there was no point in talking to Daphne. To be honest, I was sick of talking to her. I wiped a hand down my face and gave her a wary look. "What did you want to talk to me about, Daphne?"

She perked up as if she'd forgotten why she was there in the first place. Her pale delicate fingers slipped through her red locks. She flicked them this way and that before she smiled at me. "I know things haven't been easy between us—"

"Understatement of the century," I muttered.

"But I think that can change," she continued as if she hadn't heard me. "I made a mistake. I'm leaving Gabriel."

I blinked with surprise. What the...?

"Gabriel means nothing to me," she said softly.

"You left us for him," I interrupted. "I would think he meant something to you."

"I was young and impulsive. I didn't know what he was about. I was just swept up in it all. You know as well as I do that he went after me, Christian."

I laughed. Strange, I didn't feel any bitterness. If anything, I was glad she showed her true colors. "So what? A faithful wife would have said no way and told me about it. Not jumped into bed with him."

"Christian, come on."

“Come on what? What exactly are you asking for?”

“I’m asking for a second chance. You and Me. We owe it to Annie.”

"No," I stated immediately. Disgust filled my body. I’d rather stay in a cage with a poisonous snake then lie with her again. "There is nothing left between us and I don't want there to be. We're not getting back together and I wouldn't with you if you were the last woman on Earth."

Daphne narrowed her eyes. "You can either get back with me the way we both know you're going to do, or I'm going to make your life hell. I know where all your buttons are. I can press them one by one."

I stared at her incredulously. What on earth did I ever see in her? Other than her beauty, she was a vain, selfish, greedy, self-obsessed, narcissistic soulless creature. "Do you think that makes me want to be with you? If anything, that makes saying no feel so good."

"Feel how you want. You'll change your mind by the time I'm through," she snapped.

“You’ve had your say, now get out.”

She turned on her heels and stormed away.

The sound of the front door slammed and I cringed. I was heading up the stairs when I stopped. Hannah was reading to Annie and doing one of the silly animal voices perfectly.

Annie chuckled.

I stood stock-still.

Suddenly, I gripped my shirt in shock. Was I? Was I actually falling for Hannah Gray?

Chapter Twenty-Four

CHRISTIAN

"Annie, please put your shoes on," I said as she ran through the house barefoot.

"They pinch my toes!" she complained.

"They do not pinch your toes. I just brought them for you. Please, for the love of God finish getting dressed, so we can let our guests in."

Annie blew out a breath and I saw the impending tantrum coming. She hated having to wear the fancy blue dress and the shiny blue shoes with the white frilly socks. She and Hannah had picked them all out a few days ago, but for some reason, right now she wanted no part of any of it.

Hannah came around the corner, picked Annie up, and sat her on a free space on the counter. She unbuckled one shoe and slid Annie's foot into it without an ounce of resistance. Then she did the other. That done, she finger combed the curls she'd done for Annie and re-arranged her bangs until she looked like a little porcelain doll. "There. You look beautiful now."

“But I want to wear my PJs.”

“You can’t wear PJs to a party. Parties are special, so you have to dress up for them. All your friends will be dressed in their best. They’ll be photographers and everything. Don’t you want to look beautiful?”

Annie nodded. “I guess so.”

“Good. Now, why don't you go into the media room and put on some cartoons? The party is starting soon and your friends will want to watch something cool. And don't take your shoes off because someone might step on your pretty toes."

Annie gasped. "Like how the elephant stepped on the chicken’s toe?"

Hannah nodded her head. "It's very easy to do and I don't want you to get hurt, okay? As soon as the party is over, we'll kick our shoes off together and relax."

"Okay," Annie agreed seriously. "I'll go pick a movie."

"Thank you," Hannah called after her as she rushed out on her mission.

"Thank *you*," I told Hannah.

“You’re welcome,” she said with a smile.

I lifted a brow. "Are you attending my birthday party in your towel?"

Hannah shook her wet hair at me.

I grinned. "Are you trying to ruin my suit?"

She grinned back. "Don't get on my nerves and I won't shake water on your nice suit."

"You think it's nice?" I murmured, wrapping a hand around the back of her neck.

"I think it would be nicer on the floor," she whispered. "While you're on top of me."

How did she do that? Hannah always knew exactly what words would drive me absolutely insane. I kissed her and she moaned against my mouth. My hand gripped her ass and squeezed.

She swatted my hand away. "Annie, remember?"

I nodded. "Sorry. You're right. Guests should be here any minute, why don't you go get dressed?"

Hannah nodded and headed upstairs.

As soon as she'd disappeared, I heard the doorbell ring. I answered it to find a group of my friends on the doorstep.

I chatted with them as soft music played throughout the house. Waiters circulated with silver platters of canapes, and champagne started flowing like water.

I took a sip from my own flute and nearly choked when I saw Hannah.

"Are you okay?" Daniel, a business acquaintance, asked as he offered me a napkin.

"Yeah..." I cleared my throat. "I'm great. I'm really great."

Hannah was descending down the stairs like an angel wrapped in gold. The dress showed off her shoulders and hugged her curves. It was so tight she had to move slowly, so she wouldn't trip. I could tell she felt nervous about it. She didn't need to worry. It looked like she was floating.

Her sparkling blue eyes locked on mine and my heart hammered away. I'd seen her in so many things, but never something so formal. The necklace that touched her collarbone and dipped between her breasts drew my eyes. All of it made her seem like she was glowing. She reached the bottom of the stairs and smiled at me before I remembered the rest of the world existed.

"Christian West, you'll catch flies in your mouth," she teased as she walked up to me. "I take it you like the look?"

Liked it? I wanted to rip it off of her and fuck her until she couldn't do anything but moan my name from those pink lips. I wanted to hide her away and keep her to myself. Every bit of Hannah made my body kick up into a higher gear. I fucking craved this woman.

"You look beautiful," I said honestly. "Absolutely stunning."

Hannah's cheeks turned rosy. She tried to hide the fact, but I'd gotten used to her ways. Her fingers slipped up her cheeks to tuck away a stray hair.

"And who is this?" Dan asked.

"This is Annie's nanny, Hannah."

"Hello," she said shaking his hand. "Speaking of Annie, I better go check on her and her friends before they burn down the house or something. I'll be back in a minute."

She turned and I stared at her back hungrily. The dress showed off her delicious ass. I wanted to reach out and grab it, but we were in a room full of people. I had to remind myself of that, or I'd be climbing on top of her in no time.

"Happy birthday, Christian."

I turned around and didn't even try to suppress the frown that tugged at my lips.

Gabriel. He wore his hair slicked back, which made him look slimy. Like a pimp or a gigolo. He was smiling at me, but the expression in his eyes told me he dreamed of seeing me burn in hell.

"What are you doing here?" I asked.

"I came to wish you a happy birthday, of course. What kind of brother would I be if I didn't do that?"

"A self-aware one," I shot back. "In no way, do I want you to be here. Why don't you turn around and leave?"

Instead of listening, Gabriel snagged a flute of champagne from a passing waiter and delicately sipped from it as he glanced around.

I knew he was just trying to get to me, and I was a little irritated that it was working.

"Mmm... this shit is good," he said tipping the glass back and completely draining it. "I think I'll stick around for a bit," he drawled. "There's nothing better than being with family, right?"

"You and I both know we're far from family," I muttered. "If you think I'll make a scene and ruin my own party though, you're wrong. I'll let you stay here and mingle with your betters. It will be the best punishment for you."

"You're a piece of shit, you know," Gabriel said levelly.

Despite the tone, I could see that I had wounded his pride. I smiled. “Yes, I am.”

"Where's Daphne? I assume she's somewhere socializing and happy to be back home?"

I raised a brow at him. "Daphne? What the fuck are you talking about?"

"I know she came to get back with you, so let's just cut the shit. I know how much you want Daphne. You wouldn't leave her alone when we got together."

I laughed. "You couldn't pay me enough millions to get with her. Why would I want her? Actually, the real question now is why would *you* want her?"

Gabriel stepped toward me. His gaze was filled with hate.

I didn't move, didn't blink as I stared back at him. If he thought he could scare me, he was dead wrong.

"I love her," he growled. "And I want her back. I know you convinced her to leave me. Finally."

I burst out laughing in Gabriel's face.

He looked shocked as he pulled back some and I could no longer feel his breath on my face. Thank God for that. I was pretty sure I would have had to punch him if I had to deal with it much longer. At that second, however, I was much too entertained by the fact that he really thought I'd taken her from him. That he loved her, a selfish bitch like her. It was hilarious.

"What the fuck is so funny?" he snapped.

"You're right. Daphne came around here last night and asked

me to take her back. I told her to fuck off. See, Daphne doesn't love anyone, but herself. And money. Trust me, you can have her and keep her. I don't want anything to do with her."

Gabriel glared, but I was done with the situation. Why did I want to spend my party talking about the woman I would rather not see again if possible? If she weren't the mother of my child, I would take a restraining order on her.

Before he could say another word, Hannah had arrived at my side. "Annie is running that room like she's a sergeant and all of the kids are her subordinates. I swear she's a little dictator waiting to happen," she said with a laugh.

I snagged her a glass of champagne. "Have some."

Hannah shook her head. "I shouldn't. I'm watching the children."

"A few sips won't hurt," I said. "Loosen up a little."

She took a sip and smiled. "Okay, it is nice to relax a little."

Gabriel stared at us.

I willed him to go away, but he wouldn't budge.

Hannah must have felt his deep glare too because she turned around and smiled at him. She held out a hand. "Hello, I'm Annie's nanny."

"This is Gabriel, my half-brother. He's leaving," I said, my tone clipped. "Isn't that right, Gabriel?"

I watched as he reached over and shook her hand. The minute his slimy skin was touching hers I wanted to punch him in the face until he was bloody and bruised.

Hannah pulled away first. "Nice to meet you," she said quietly. Her mouth was set in a straight line and a nerve jumped in her temple. She looked like she was ready to sock him one.

Just seeing that she was upset about him, because of what he'd done to me, gave me comfort.

“Christian, could I talk to you for a minute?” she asked.

“Of course.” Taking her elbow, I started to guide her away from my brother.

“Have fun, Christian,” Gabriel called.

I ignored him.

We moved through the party to put as much distance between him and us as possible. Once we’d made it across the room, I let go of her and reached for a glass from a circulating tray of champagne. I couldn’t think of a better time to have a drink. I raised a brow at her and she seemed to realize that I was waiting.

“Oh,” she said quickly. “I didn’t actually need anything I just wanted to get you away from him. Sorry. Did I read it wrong? Your face had a ‘get me the hell out of here’ vibe.”

I burst out laughing. “Was it that pronounced?”

She grinned. “I don’t know if anyone else would have noticed it, but to me? Oh, yeah. You had that little nerve on the left side of your mouth that does its own thing when you’re not happy.”

My chest clenched. How had she’d learned so much about me? Hannah had come into my life and changed everything. I couldn’t remember the last time someone had remembered something so minute about me. My ex-wife certainly never took the time. "You know you're amazing, right?"

I watched her eyes light up as she sipped at her champagne. We walked the party together, chatting and mingling between spurts of her checking on the children. I couldn't think of a single person I'd rather spend time with.

Chapter Twenty-Five

HANNAH

The party lingered on and on and I didn't realize how late or how much drinking, Christian's friends could do. By the time it got late, most of the parents who'd brought children had sleepy kids on their hands. One by one, they carried them out and let their drivers take them home.

Annie had passed out a while ago, curled up with her little black shoes on the couch.

I pushed her curls from her face and smiled. She'd done a good job, never taking them off and being the boss of the others. I knew she'd make a good leader someday. Even I was impressed by the way she negotiated peace between the Bronson twins and kept the room running smoothly when I stepped out. She'd had fun and even made new friends.

"Come on, Princess."

I slipped off her shoes and picked her up. She automatically wrapped her arms around my neck almost choking me as I carried her out of the room.

Christian caught sight of me moving across the party with her in my arms and stopped me. "Let me take her."

"No, no you go ahead. I'll just get her upstairs and into bed."

Christian shook his head. "You look great in that dress, but you can barely move and I don't think you can navigate the stairs like that. Besides, you've been working the whole night. I admire your dedication, but you need to take a little break. Go on, I'll be right back."

I felt a little bad about Christian having to take care of things at his own party, but I let it go because he was definitely right about the dress. He set up an account for me at an expensive boutique and insisted that I buy something that I would never have been able to afford. I nearly died when I saw the price of the clothes there, but he had called me on my cell and told me either I got myself a dress or he was going to buy it himself.

Put like that, the little gold number had called to me right away and I'd picked it immediately. The way his jaw dropped tonight when he saw me confirmed that it was definitely a great purchase.

I watched the two of them disappear up the stairs. Christian kissed her gently before they disappeared from sight and I sighed contentedly. The night couldn't have gone better. I grabbed a flute and glanced around the party. As nice as everyone had been to me, I wanted a little alone time to myself.

Navigating my way around and smiling politely, I decided to go outside to the gardens. The garden was one of my favorite places at night. The floral scent always made me happy. As soon as I entered it, I could smell the night blooming Jasmine and I smiled. A crescent moon lit the sky up above just a bit, and I could have stayed there forever.

"You two seem very close."

I jumped at the sound of the voice and spilled some champagne down my dress. Light droplets darkened the golden fabric and I quickly attempted to brush them off. When I glanced up, I saw Gabriel.

He had one hand in his pocket while he looked me up and down in a way that made me shift from foot to foot.

"Who?" I asked, even though I knew exactly what he meant.

"You and Christian," he said as he sauntered forward. "Is there something there?"

I stared at him. Why did he care? The more I heard about Gabriel the less I liked him, but dealing with him up close and personal gave me the creeps. He was a good looking guy, but he was intimidating in an almost predatory way. "I suppose," I answered with a polite smile. "He's my boss."

"Just your boss?" he mused.

Something in his voice alerted me to an immediate danger. *Why the hell did I come out here alone?* I frowned. "Well, he *is* my boss."

"Then he won't mind if I do this," he said taking a step closer.

"What?" I stared wide eyed with shock as he grabbed my arm and tried to drag me deeper into the garden.

At first, my mind went blank. I couldn't even understand

what he was doing. Then my brain came back online and screamed one thing.

Run.

Chapter Twenty-Six

HANNAH

I couldn't run. I could hardly walk in this dress, let alone run. But I could scream. Even as I opened my mouth to do that, he shoved his hand against my mouth, while his other hand tightened on my arm. With a hard look on his face, he yanked me away from the party, away from Christian.

In my panic, I dropped my glass of champagne and it shattered on the stone path. We were in the furthest reaches of the garden, a place that was darker and away from the house. My heart thudded in my chest.

What was I going to do?

Everything in me screamed to get away from him. I somehow knew he wanted to teach Christian some kind of lesson by using me. I wanted no part of it. I tried to struggle, to pull away, but he yanked me against his body so I couldn't move at all. I could smell his aftershave.

"Hold still," he growled.

His breath caressed my ear making me shudder with fear.

"Don't make this harder than it has to be."

I elbowed him in the side, but it did nothing. He moved faster, his hand on my thigh as he grabbed my dress. I heard the fabric rip sharply.

I had a crazy thought then. Instead of worrying about what he was doing to me, I started to get angry about what was happening to my dress. I'd brought it for Christian, to make him smile the way he did when I walked down the stairs. Now, Gabriel was ruining it. I became scared. What if Christian never looked at me the same way again? What if his touch turned me into someone Christian couldn't even look at anymore? Like those men who leave their wives and girlfriends when they have been raped, because they can't cope with the guilt. Angry tears flowed down my face.

I didn't understand Gabriel. How could he want to hurt Christian so badly? It was one thing to steal his ex-wife, but this was horrible.

My head spun. I wanted to get away from him, but Gabriel was too strong.

His hand touched my bare thigh and I screamed against his palm. It was slicked with sweat and hot. I wanted to bite him but he was smart enough to keep from pressing it against my teeth. No matter what I did, how I tried to twist and turn, he kept me locked against his body with his hot breath on my neck and his voice sending shivers of disgust up my spine.

"I told you to just hold still. This isn't about you," he hissed. "Christian needs to learn what happens when you fuck with me. I've had enough of his bullshit."

“Let me go!” I shouted against his hand.

“Not until I’m done with you. Go ahead, keep fighting me. You’re just making this harder on yourself.”

I shook my head as his hand traveled upward. The last thing I wanted was that slimy, disgusting bastard touching me anywhere. My skin crawled as I tried to yank myself away from him. I felt his fingers on the edge of my panties. I jerked, but that only made his fingers enter my panties. I began to rock my body as hard as I could, so he would have to fight even to hold me in place.

Then I heard a movement and my eyes swung in that direction.

Christian yanked Gabriel away from me. Gabriel almost fell, but Christian wouldn’t allow that. Without a word, he balled up his fist and punched him in the face.

His brother reeled back and held his nose as blood seeped from between his fingers.

“Get the fuck out of here and don’t ever show your face to me again. This is nothing compared to what I’ll do to you if I *ever* see you again.”

Gabriel glared at the two of us, but he scrambled and disappeared like the coward he really was.

As soon as he was gone, I crumpled to the ground. My dress was in tatters around me and that brute had almost got his fingers inside me.

Christian wrapped his arms around me.

I clung to him. “He ruined my dress!” I wailed.

"It's just a dress. I'll buy ten more," he said hoarsely.

"I bought it for you." I sobbed.

"It's okay, It's okay," he repeated again and again.

My tears began to fall in earnest. My body shook and I couldn't stop for a long time.

Christian didn't rush me. He ran his hand over my hair and back as he held me so tightly I could barely breathe.

It was just what I needed. I finally wiped my eyes. "I think I messed up your suit," I said quietly.

"It's just a suit," he said as he wrapped an arm around my shoulders. "You're more important than that."

I clutched the front of my dress and leaned against him as we walked back to the house. He grasped my hand and placed a kiss on the back of it. The simple gesture warmed me and made me feel safe and whole again. I'd been scared that he would reject me after I had been touched by Gabriel, but that wasn't the case at all. I could feel how much he wanted to comfort me.

"I don't think I can go in. My dress is all ruined," I said as I showed him the rip.

"We'll take you in the back way and you can go upstairs to my room. I'll clear everyone out. I'm done partying, anyway."

"Okay." I nodded and started to walk off.

He pulled me back. His thumb swiped underneath my eyes and he cradled my cheeks in his palms. "Are you okay?"

"Of course."

"Hannah."

I stared up at him and slowly shook my head. "No, not really. He scared me," I whispered. "I don't want him near me again."

"He won't be," Christian promised. "I'll make sure of that."

Chapter Twenty-Seven

CHRISTIAN

I bent my head and pressed my lips to her forehead. She leaned into me, soaking me in before she slowly pulled away. We got her quietly into the house before I thanked everyone and abruptly ended the party. Everything could be dealt with tomorrow. I wanted to get to her as quickly as possible.

When I slipped upstairs, I heard the shower running in the bathroom. I stripped off and joined her. She quickly took my arms and wrapped them around her as she leaned against me. We didn't say a word, just took our time as I washed her hair and body.

Why didn't I realize it before?

I'd been so hell-bent on keeping any sort of emotions out of our fun time that I hadn't realized just how much I cared for her. Seeing her with Gabriel, knowing that he could have hurt her had sparked something in me. I would do anything for Hannah. She meant the world to me.

I turned the water off and stepped out to grab us towels. I

threw one carelessly on around my waist, then I took my time drying her off bit by bit until her skin was rosy.

She glanced up at me as I stood up and brushed my fingers against her cheek.

“Better?” I asked.

Hannah nodded and I saw her real smile peeking through. “Yeah,” she answered. “Much better.”

I kissed her deeply and she gripped my arms tightly. I kissed her until her body relaxed in my arms. When we pulled back from each other, the muscles in her face and shoulder had softened too and I knew that she was finally beginning to shake off the traumatic incident, but it could still take a little while.

“Hannah, I will always protect you. No matter what,” I said quietly.

“I know you will,” she whispered.

My chest swelled with pride. As long as she knew I would take care of her, what more could I ask for? I wrapped the towel around her tightly and lifted her up into my arms. She leaned her head on my chest as I carried her into my bedroom. I didn’t plan on spending a single minute that night doing anything but comforting and pampering her.

“What’s this?” I asked as I pointed to a dark mark on her wrist.

“I think he bruised me,” she muttered.

I was pissed off all over again. “I should have kept hitting the bastard. Maybe it would have knocked some sense into his thick head.”

Hannah shook her head. "No, I don't think violence is ever the answer. Although, I can't say I really blame you. I wanted to poke him in the eye." She reached up and stroked my cheek. "I'm sorry you've had to deal with him all this time. I can't even imagine the hell that he's put you through."

My chest tightened. How could she be concerned about me right now? How could she be sad for me when she was the one who had been hurt? She was the one that had just been through an ordeal, not me. Yet, there she was still worrying about me, still caring about me in a way that no one else had.

Hannah wasn't like anyone I'd ever met before.

She saw so much and said just the right words to make everything okay again. I knew that's why Annie loved her and I suppose that's why I did too.

"Stop thinking about me," I told her. "Think about yourself."

"I like thinking about you," she answered. "You need someone to look out for you too. No one does that."

My chest swelled even more and it took everything not to climb on top of her and kiss her a million times until I could erase what Gabriel did to her. I planted a kiss on her head and smiled at her.

Hannah smiled softly when I did.

Damn, I knew there was definitely something more going on here.

I couldn't deny it anymore.

Chapter Twenty-Eight

HANNAH

I woke up the next morning in my own bed. Christian had insisted I sleep with him, but I couldn't do it. Not with Annie prowling the house early in the mornings. As much as I adored him, and no matter how badly I'd wanted to stay wrapped up in his arms all night, I knew what things were between us, and Annie didn't need to see any part of it. I didn't want her to get her hopes up, or be upset.

Either way, it could end everything and I didn't want that.

It may have been scraps from Christian's table, but I loved what I had.

Spending the night with Christian while he massaged and caressed every inch of me had only confirmed that more. He hadn't tried to do anything beyond kiss and hold me and I loved him for it. I wanted him more for it.

Get it together, Hannah.

I knew I had to stop thinking about him in this way, or I'd drive myself crazy, but I almost couldn't help myself. I felt so safe when I was with him. I knew that he'd do anything to protect me now. Turning over, I groaned into my pillow. Then I forced myself to stop thinking about him and got up.

A brand new day stretched in front of me.

A knock on my door went from quiet to long and loud and I knew that it was Annie. I smiled and slipped from the bed, wrapped myself in a robe, and padded to the door.

When I opened it, she smiled up at me in her PJ's with her hair all adorably messy.

"Good morning," I said. "You're up early."

"We go shopping today."

"Yes, we do." I grinned. "Right after we put on clothes, brush our teeth, and have breakfast."

She groaned. "Can't we do all of that stuff later?"

"Should we go in our robes and PJ's?" I asked.

Annie's little face lit up. "Can we?"

"You know we can't." I laughed and messed up her hair even more.

She giggled. "Stop it!"

"Fine," I said. "Let's get ready to start the day, hmm?"

"You two have fun," Christian said, as he walked out of his bedroom fully dressed and looking drop dead hot. "I'll see you both after work."

"Okay, Daddy," Annie said as she ran over and gave him a tight hug.

"I second that *okay daddy* bit," I said and I winked at him.

He laughed. A happy sound.

"Daddy, give Hannah a hug too."

"A hug for Hannah?" Christian asked as he pulled me into a bear hug.

I slapped his arm until he let me go.

"We're going to the mall to go shopping," Annie announced.

"Great. Bring something back for me."

"Okay," she said happily and ran off to get ready.

When Christian was sure she was gone, he yanked me back against his body and kissed me so hard my knees buckled.

"What was that for?" I asked breathlessly.

"Just felt like it."

I groaned. "Can't you kiss me when I don't have morning breath?"

"It's always amazing kissing you."

I felt my cheeks bloom with heat. Sometimes he could say the sweetest things and it always threw me off. I walked him to the door to wave him off.

Just before he walked out of the door, Christian slipped me a credit card and whispered in my ear to go crazy. Stark raving crazy or he would be disappointed in me.

I looked down at the card. It had my name on it. I looked up and he winked at me. I didn't know about stark raving crazy, but we were definitely going to have some fun as Annie was outgrowing some of her clothes and I was sure she could use an update.

I got myself and Annie ready for our girls' day out then we drove to the mall.

Annie was so excited she took my hand and practically dragged me through the entrance. She was surprisingly strong. We stopped in front of the toy store and Annie's eyes went wide as she took in all the possibilities.

"Clothes first," I reminded her. "And then toys."

"Aww, can't we do toys first?"

She looked super cute and I was sorely tempted, but I knew what would happen if I let her have her way. We'd be in the toy store all day and then she wouldn't feel like shopping for clothes. It was enough to make me want to cave, but I straightened my spine and shook my head. "Toys after. Come on, don't you want new clothes? I'm sure there are some cute PJ's too."

"New PJ's?" she asked curiously.

"Yeah, the kind with animal ears and tails."

"Cool beans!"

I laughed as she swiftly abandoned the idea of toy shopping for new clothes. At least, I could redirect her when I needed to.

We walked into a kiddie store and her eyes lit up as she led me over to one of the racks. "Look at this dress. It's so cute!"

I smiled as I pushed through the rack. "I like this one better."

We went through the clothes together and pulled out things we liked. I draped them over my arm one by one before I went back to rummaging in the racks. By the time I glanced up, I was sure we were going to spend a fortune. "Annie, we need to try some of these things on to make sure they fit. I think we should. Annie?"

I glanced around. She had been right by my side the whole time, but now she was just gone. My heart started to race as I turned around and started to look around for her. I peeked between the racks and around the store, but I couldn't find her.

"Annie? Annie!"

I threw the clothes over my arm on the floor and scrambled frantically as I tried to find her. I ran around the store in a panic, but I couldn't see her. I ran out of the store and started to look for her. She was nowhere to be seen.

I ran up to one person after another. "Have you seen a little girl in a pink top with a yellow elephant on the front and blue jeans?"

No one had seen her.

The mall was full of people and I couldn't see her anywhere. Tears sprung to my eyes as I moved through the wide space. I could tell I was unraveling. This was the worst thing that could possibly have happened.

Pull it together for Annie.

I forced myself to keep moving. I needed to find her now. Oh, God. Oh, God. I need to find a security guard. They have cameras.

I needed to call the police right away. If someone had taken her then the sooner I called, the better. I dug into my pocket and pulled out my cellphone when my ears picked up a familiar sound.

Annie's little voice calling to me.

"Come on, Annie. Let's go."

I whirled around and my eyes landed on Daphne. *What the fuck?* She was dragging Annie through the mall and frowning furiously. Annie looked like she'd rather be anywhere, but by her mother's side.

I stalked up to them and crossed my arms in front of my chest. "Daphne," I said sharply. "What are you doing? Annie's supposed to be with me."

The woman looked me up and down. "Oh? I didn't know I needed permission to have access to my daughter." She laughed. An ugly sound. "Besides, you obviously can't do a good job at keeping an eye on her. What were you thinking letting her wander off like that?" She lifted her chin at me.

I bristled with annoyance. It was clear to me that she had taken Annie away on purpose. Probably just to watch me squirm and have something on Christian about the way Annie was being taken care of. "Annie, come here," I said and held out my hand.

Immediately, she yanked her hand from Daphne's grip and ran to me. Slipping her hand into mine, she pressed her body against me.

I gave her hand a little squeeze to let her know that everything would be okay. If Annie hadn't been standing there, I knew I would have yelled at Daphne for pulling such a stupid stunt, but I didn't want to upset Annie.

"I have things to do anyway," Daphne sniffed. "You can take her home."

I was going to do that anyway, bitch.

In my life, I tried not to think badly about anyone, or talk badly about them, but honestly Daphne was in a league all on her own. I could see the way she used Annie to try to get what she wanted and it made my stomach turn. "Thanks," I said sarcastically.

"I heard about you," Daphne called after I started to turn to leave. "Gabriel told me all about how you and Christian were at the party. How close you were."

"And?" I snapped.

"And I want you to know that you're nothing. You stay the hell away from Christian or there will be serious consequences."

I scoffed. "Are you threatening me?"

"Threatening? No. I'm telling you exactly what's going to happen if you decide to keep going after Christian."

Before I could say a word, she turned around and stalked off on her high heels as if she'd just done something great.

I gritted my teeth. How could anyone be that awful? I didn't get why she was so focused on Christian when he clearly wanted nothing to do with her.

I glanced down at Annie. "Do you want to pick up some lunch and go home?" I asked quietly.

Annie nodded. She still seemed to be a bit dazed. "Yeah," she whispered. "I want to go home."

I took her hand as we headed for the exit to the mall. She refused to let go of my hand the entire time and I kept glancing at her to make sure she was okay.

Chapter Twenty-Nine

HANNAH

The drive home was quiet for once.

Annie didn't talk my ear off. Instead, she stared ahead and kicked the back of the seat quietly. For such a young child, it was easy to see there was a lot on her mind. I wanted to say something to comfort her, but I felt like I should hold back and wait until she was ready to come to me.

We pulled up to the house and I helped her out then we slipped inside. As soon as I shut the door behind us, she turned around and hugged my legs tightly.

I quickly crouched down and pulled her into my arms.

She squeezed me harder.

"I wish you were my Mommy," she sniffled and buried her face in my shoulder.

My heart clenched. I didn't want to say the wrong thing, but I could understand why she didn't want Daphne to be her mother. She constantly used her and threw her away when it didn't serve her. It made me so angry. Annie was such a special child and to not be fully appreciated by her mother hurt.

"It's okay, sweetie," I whispered quietly as I stroked her hair.

"Can't you stay with Daddy and me forever?"

My eyes watered and I knew I was close to bawling my eyes out, but I couldn't stop myself. I loved being around Annie. She was the light I needed to be happy, even if Daphne didn't see that. I didn't plan on going anywhere, but I knew that wasn't up to me, and I couldn't feed her false hope. "What do you say we go get all cleaned up and then we watch something together, hmm?" I asked after I'd wiped my eyes quickly. "Does that sound good?"

Annie looked at me sadly but she didn't push it. Just nodded.

I knew this was as good as it could be at the moment.

We ended up relaxing on the couch and even eating dinner there. She fell asleep on my lap as I stroked her hair and stared at the TV without really watching it.

"Hey."

I glanced up at Christian in the doorway. "Hey," I whispered. "She's out."

"I see. Sorry, I'm late I had a meeting run really long. Is everything okay?"

I shook my head a little. "Can we talk? After you put Annie to bed?"

Christian nodded and gently lifted her from my lap then took her upstairs.

I followed behind.

He settled her into the bed and tucked her in.

She mumbled in her sleep, clutched her pillow, then was completely out of it again.

We both slipped out of the room and Christian shut the door behind him. Then we walked into his room and only once that door was closed did I finally sag and allow how much the whole thing had bothered me to take over.

"What's wrong?" Christian asked as he gripped my shoulders and gave them a squeeze.

"We ran into Daphne at the mall. And by ran into I mean she lured Annie away just to see me lose my shit. And then when I caught up with them, she warned me to stay away from you or she's going to... I don't know come after me, or something," I cried, tears gathering in my eyes and rolling helplessly down my face.

“What?”

“I was so terrified. I thought she’d been taken by a pedophile. Oh, my God, Christian you don’t know how afraid I was! It was the most frightening feeling in the whole world. I would rather have Gabriel rape me than feel that again. I don’t know what she is going to tell you, but I swear I wasn’t careless with Annie. I love Annie with all my heart.” I couldn’t speak anymore and I began to sob like a baby.

"Fuck. She’s such a bitch," he spat.

“You believe me?”

He put his hands on either side of my cheeks. “Yes, I believe you.”

I felt a little better.

"You know I'm going to protect you no matter what, right?"

I nodded. "Yeah, I remember," I said as I reached up and covered his hands with my own.

"I'll have a chat with her, so don't worry anymore, okay? I know how to handle her."

I nodded. "Okay."

"You feel better now?"

"Yes, but I've got something else to get off my chest."

"Go on."

I sniffed. "Annie said something kind of funny today and I didn't know how to respond."

"What did she say?"

"She wished I was her Mommy and she wanted me to stay here forever," I said, glancing up at him. "I didn't know what to say. I don't want her to hate her mom, so I didn't say anything negative, but I couldn't think of anything positive to say either. It just felt like bullshit on my tongue, and I couldn't lie to her. Why are you smiling?"

"You did well," he said. "You can't lie to a kid. They'll pick up on it in an instant."

I pursed my lips. "Well, I'm glad then that I did the right thing."

"You did well not to lie to her."

I relaxed a little at his words. At least I knew I hadn't

screwed her up for life in some way. As much as I knew how to be a nanny, I'd never been a parent. And I'd never had anyone tell me they wished I was their mother. It was surreal.

Christian stroked my cheek.

I then put my focus back on him. That weird smile hadn't left his lips and I stared up at him confused. What was going on inside his head? "What?" I finally asked.

"Would you like to be my girlfriend?"

Chapter Thirty

HANNAH

I stared at Christian like he'd lost his mind.

I heard the words but it was like my brain couldn't process them. *His girlfriend? He wanted me to be his girlfriend?* I couldn't make sense of those words in my head so instead, I stared and stuttered, "U-umm..."

Christian chuckled underneath his breath. "Are you going to say something?"

"I'm not really sure I know how words work anymore," I mumbled. I didn't think he would ever want me to be his girlfriend. He'd made it clear right from the start that he didn't want a real relationship and as much as I'd hated it, I also knew I couldn't force him into anything. So, to hear him say that he wanted me to be his girlfriend completely floored me. "Are you serious?"

"Very serious," he said as he took my hands.

"How do you feel about me?" I asked.

Christian's thumb caressed my cheek. "I feel things for you

that I've never felt for anyone before," he said. "Not for Daphne, not for anyone. So I want to give us a shot. We deserve that much. What do you think?"

I smiled up at him. Of course, that's what I wanted. All I'd ever thought about when it came to him was how much I wanted to be in his life. And Annie's. I adored both of them so much I couldn't imagine being without them. "I think that's the best idea you've ever had. Well, besides the one where you asked me to sleep with you." I laughed nervously. "Of course, I want to be your girlfriend."

Christian's smile grew until he looked happy enough to burst. He palmed my cheeks and swooped down on my lips. The little peck turned into a wildfire. Our lips moved together hard, our breaths whipping into fast pants. His hands moved first and yanked my clothes off as I went for his.

The terrible tension I'd felt all day disappeared when he was holding and touching me like he just couldn't get enough. I moaned against his lips as his tongue slipped into my mouth. He explored and tasted me until I couldn't stand it anymore. I wanted to feel him, every inch of him.

I pushed him hard onto the bed and he fell back in surprise. I chuckled as I licked the crease of his neck and nipped at it with my teeth. That drew a long, passionate moan from his mouth and I wanted to hear it again and again.

He chuckled. "Did you want me that bad?"

"You have no idea."

I couldn't imagine not wanting Christian. His hard, muscled body pressed against mine was something that I could never get enough of. My fingers scraped down his chest, long and slow as he arched his back and pressed up into my hands. He trusted me, that much was clear and he wanted me like no other. I couldn't imagine being with anyone and having them want me the way he did. It was deeper than anything I'd ever had before.

"Hannah," he groaned.

"Shhhh." I kissed down along his chest over his belly and between each of his muscular thighs. The scent of his arousal was strong and heady. It drew me in and made me want to climb on top of him and ride him until I'd had my fill and then some. Instead, I slid my tongue over the insides of his thighs and over his balls.

Christian sucked in a breath. I glanced up at him and he locked eyes with me. I let my tongue drag over his flesh before I sucked one ball and then the other into my mouth.

His body bowed and he tensed. "Hannah," he managed to choke out.

"Not done yet," I said as I released his balls and dragged my tongue back up his extremely rigid shaft.

"You're being greedy tonight. Does this mean you're happy?"

"Mmhmm..." I moaned. "Very happy." I opened my mouth and swallowed the whole of his cock before he could say another word. The only sound I received was a deep moan and that was more than enough to make me grin inwardly and slide my mouth downwards until he was nestled neatly in my throat. I swallowed around him, my throat constricting and tightening as he threw back his head and bucked upward into my throat.

The more he bucked, the more I swallowed and moaned

while my fingertips massaged his balls. Until I was sure he was going crazy. He was on the edge and ready to explode, but every time he came close, I pulled away and started all over again. I wanted him right on the edge of the razor blade, and I wanted him to feel as good as I did hearing him say that he had feelings for me.

My body was in overdrive mode.

Heat swept over me and I was so wet I could feel it dripping down my thighs. I crawled up his body and straddled his lap as I glanced down at him.

Christian reached up and grasped my breasts, tweaking and pinching my nipples.

I moaned and bit down on my lip.

He knew exactly how to touch me.

His hand stroked down along my chest and stomach. Then his fingers pushed between my legs. He rubbed around my clit in little circles until my breath caught in my throat. If I was ready before, I was dying for him now.

His fingers shifted and two of them pushed into my wetness. He stroked my spot.

"Fuck," I groaned. "That feels amazing."

“Shhh,” he whispered when I cried out.

I whimpered underneath my breath. He was right about keeping quiet, but he made it so hard to do when he knew exactly how to work himself inside me and make me a squirming, moaning mess.

I cupped my own breasts. My fingers pinched at my already

hard nipples as he watched entranced. He fingered me until I was too wet to think straight. "No more," I moaned. "I need you."

"I need you too." Christian rolled us sideway so I was on my back and he was on top of me. My legs wrapped around his waist automatically as he reached between us and froze.

"Christian?" I asked quietly. "What's wrong?"

"Nothing's wrong."

"Then why did you stop?"

"I forgot to stop on the way home and buy more condoms. We used the last one last night. It's okay. We can do other things," he mumbled.

Christian started to shift away, but I squeezed my thighs around his waist. "I'm clean," I said as I pulled him back in place. "I was tested after my ex and I haven't been with anyone since."

He looked down at me. "Same with Daphne. I got everything checked just in case. Are you sure though?"

I smiled up at him. "I don't think I've ever been surer about anything in my life."

Christian's lips captured mine and my body trembled with nervous anticipation. He didn't waste time holding back or teasing me. Instead, he rubbed the head of his cock against me, up and down, until I squirmed and practically begged to feel it inside of me.

When he slipped inside of me, I cried out. It wasn't the same as it was with a condom. The feeling of his skin buried inside me made me moan and clench around him. Heat met heat and he thrust inside of me slowly as if he was savoring the feeling too.

Each thrust rubbed against my walls and made me moan. I wrapped my arms around his neck and tangled my tongue with his until I didn't know whether I was coming or going. We rocked and shifted against the sheets.

"Christian," I moaned. "I love this, but please go faster. I'm dying here."

"Faster?" he asked as he peppered my neck, chest, and shoulders with kisses. "Why would I do that?"

"Please," I begged.

"That's better, baby"

I melted at the endearment.

He picked up speed and thrust inside of me harder and harder until my back arched into a bow. My breasts pressed against his body as he gazed into my eyes with complete adoration. I held my breath, too excited and too close to breathe. "Kiss me," I whispered. "Kiss me."

I could feel the way his cock twitched and jumped inside of me as he rocked back and forth. His breathing turned into low, growling groans, as he did just that, kissed the breath from me. I knew he wasn't far either. I waited to feel him fill me up at the same time that I came.

It didn't take long. He pushed himself deeper and I cried out as my body tensed and shook with the rolling waves. I came so hard it stole the sound from my lips. The first wave was hardly gone when another began. This time it was stronger and more ferocious. Electricity flooded my senses and I kissed him as I came a second time.

It pushed him over the edge then he pulled back and painted my belly with his cum.

Both of us were gone as he rolled off of me and laid by my side.

I willed the world to stop spinning so I wouldn't lose it.

Christian kissed my neck. "I'll get you cleaned up in two minutes," he promised.

"I don't even care," I mumbled. "Leave me here until I die."

Christian kissed my cheek. "I can't do that. I wouldn't leave you anywhere... You're my girlfriend."

My entire body flushed. Just hearing him say those words sent me into hyper drive, and I wanted to bask in it. I touched his cheek and kissed along his strong, stubble lined jaw. "I think I'm going to like being your girlfriend." I smiled.

"I sure hope so."

Chapter Thirty-One

HANNAH

Christian's girlfriend.

I still couldn't quite believe it was true. Just thinking about it made me feel tingly all over. I rolled over in his arms and kissed the tip of his nose. He wiggled it like a cute little bunny. Maybe that was what I'd call him. Bunny. I was sure he'd hate it and try to change my mind, but that was half of the fun.

I poked his nose again and he sniffed before he licked my finger. I cringed and ewwed as I tried to roll away from him, but he wrapped his hand around my waist and refused to let me go. His lips pressed into the back of my neck as I tried to escape. I couldn't get free.

And... I loved it.

He fucked me again and again. But the last time, it was more like making love.

I slipped out of the room before Annie woke up because I wasn't quite comfortable having her find out that we were sharing the same bed yet. I wanted her to have stability. Christian agreed.

All I could think about when he was gone to work that morning was doing something special for him. He'd gone out of his comfort zone to ask me out and I wanted to repay him. Annie and I hung out until around noon when she was supposed to meet her grandparents.

Usually, she clung to me like it was the end of the world, but seeing Christian's parents made her dash off and disappear into the house before I could hardly say goodbye. I smiled at her independence. It was a good sign.

I didn't go back to the house like I could have. Instead, I pulled up to Christian's office and pulled out the basket lunch I'd packed for him. It had all of his favorites, a bottle of wine, two glasses and even some dessert. And if he didn't have a sweet tooth, I would gladly offer myself as an end of meal snack.

A grin spread across my lips as I glanced in the side mirror of the car. My hair was tucked in place perfectly, my dress was neat, and my heart was beating like a drum. I couldn't wait to see the smile on his face. I nervously toyed with the handle of the basket as I rode the elevator up to the top floor. My heels clicked along the floor to his secretary's desk before I waited for her to be off of the phone.

"Can I help you?" she asked.

"Yes. I'm looking for Christian."

The woman looked me up and down. There was almost a pitying look on her face.

I shrank back a bit. *Why is she looking at me like that?*

"Mr. West is busy at the moment," she said finally.

"Oh," I replied. I could feel my face falling. "Did he step out for a minute? I can wait if he's going to come right back. I know he's always in meetings."

I heard a sound from behind the woman and I frowned. It had to be from Christian's office. His name was displayed in gold and black on the door. My teeth worried my lip before I glanced back at her.

"Mr. West's ex-wife is speaking to him," she finally blurted out. "She's been in there for a while, so I don't know if you should wait."

"Oh," I said. He did say he would talk to her. Maybe that was what he was doing with her.

"Yeah, she's been here every day this week."

I nodded slowly, but it felt like someone else had gained control of my head and was nodding it for me. *She'd been here all week?* I couldn't understand why Christian wouldn't tell me that. I poured my heart and soul out to him. My belly clenched. The splendid special moment when he'd asked me to be his girlfriend rang hollow once I knew that he'd been lying to me about her.

The old me would have turned and fled.

But I loved him.

That thought alone made me change the way I would normally react. Instead of running away, I stalked past his secretary's desk. The jealousy and anger I felt fueled me as I grabbed the knob, ignored her feeble protests, and flung his office door open.

My mind told me that I would catch them in the act.

I steeled myself against it. I was getting ready to see him cheating on me when I stumbled into the office. Instead of finding her in his lap, or draped over his desk with him pounding her from behind the way he did me on his desk at home, I found him pushing her away from him, and damn near growling with fury.

"Get the hell out of my office," he seethed. "Before I call security and have you thrown out. We're finished. Why can't you get that through your damn thick head! Stop coming to my office, stop coming to my house, stop stalking Hannah. Just stop, damn it. I'm done with you. Get out!"

I blinked in surprise. His secretary was wrong... this wasn't a sweet reunion between the two exes. I clutched my dress in my fist and felt tears well up in my eyes. For a moment there, I'd doubted him, but he never had any intention of leaving my side. If it was possible, I loved him even more.

Daphne snatched up her bag and spun on her heels.

When her eyes landed on me, I felt cold shoot through my body. I could see the hatred in her gaze.

She stalked past me then she stopped to glare at me. "Fuck you, bitch. You deserve each other!" she snapped before she stormed out of Christian's office and slammed the door behind her.

Chapter Thirty-Two

CHRISTIAN

I hadn't noticed Hannah had walked in. I'd been too focused on Daphne. Well, more like too focused on getting her the fuck away from me. I saw the hurt look on Hannah's face, but something else too, that I couldn't describe.

I walked over to her and took her hands. "Hannah, I didn't mean for you to see any of that. I should have told you," I said as I shook my head. "I don't know what the hell... Are you okay?"

Hannah nodded slowly. "Why didn't you tell me that she had been here so much? I thought that maybe you were still seeing her for a minute there."

I nodded. "I know, I know. It's just that I don't feel anything for Daphne. I haven't in a long time. When she kept popping up here, I didn't think to bring it up because she isn't important. Every time she showed her face here, I just wanted it over and all I could think about was your face and getting home to you." I shook my head. "I'm sorry I didn't tell you, but only because it was so unimportant to me. To us."

She moved forward and kissed me deeply.

My body relaxed. I knew that with that kiss she was letting it all go. I was beating myself up for not mentioning Daphne had been stopping by.

Hannah kissed me like she just didn't care, like she couldn't get enough.

I came up for air, panting and disheveled.

She still leaned toward me, her eyes closed. Suddenly, her eyelids flutter open. Then she smiled happily at me.

I moved to my desk, picked up the two tickets and walked back to her. "Look at these," I said as I pressed them into her hand.

"What's this?" she murmured as she opened the envelope. She gasped. "Does that say what I think it says?"

I nodded. "Tickets to the Palais Garnier in Paris. Ever since you told me you wanted to go there one night, I've wanted to get these tickets for you. What do you think?"

She stared at the tickets in surprise before she looked up at me with teary eyes. "You did this for me?"

"Of course. You're my girl." I smiled. "I want you to have the best of everything."

Hannah wrapped her arms around my neck and squeezed me tightly. I let her cling to me for as long as she wanted to. I loved seeing how happy she was.

When she pulled back, she wiped her eyes and grinned. "I

can't believe this. I can't wait. Oh, wait, what about Annie? Is she going to want to be on a plane that long?" she asked.

"Annie is going to stay with my parents. They want some extra time with her and I figured it would be the perfect time to get out and have some fun. Besides, we won't be schlepping it to an airport and climbing on a plane. We'll be taking my private jet. Quiet, all the room you could hope for, a personal chef and a bed just for the two of us."

Hannah stared at me for a minute. Then she kissed me hard.

I laughed, happy that she was so excited. My lips moved against hers.

When she pulled back, she stared up at me with starry eyes.

I loved that about her. How starry her eyes could get. Hannah might not ask me for much, but when I surprised her with something she really loved, she gave me a look as if she could drown in my eyes.

"Thank you," she whispered. "Seriously, this is the best thing that's ever happened to me. I love it."

I smiled. "I'm falling for you more and more. I don't want to hide that from you. I want you to know how much I care about you. I know I've been slow in getting there, but I can promise it's getting better second by second, baby."

"Really?" she asked. "I feel the same way... like this is getting deeper every day and I don't even know what to do about that."

I grinned and pulled her into my arms. That's exactly what I wanted to hear. There was something completely different about Hannah... from any other woman I'd ever met. She was beautiful, confident, kind, strong, and all around amazing. She was also so selfless when it came to the people she cared about. Why she ever agreed to just sex then never pushed for more, showed how selfless she really was. I couldn't imagine spending time away from her.

"You don't have to be Annie's nanny anymore," I told her. "You don't have to work for me and she can have her wish of you being her mother. I think she's going to be excited."

Hannah laughed. "Excited? She's going to lose her mind about me staying with you guys permanently. You know how she is."

I could see how happy Hannah was about that. She and Annie had gotten so close that I couldn't stand the idea of them being away from each other either. Annie deserved someone who loved her and wanted to be around her as much as I did. Hannah was clearly the perfect choice for that. For everything in our lives.

Chapter Thirty-Three

HANNAH

I couldn't be happier hearing Christian say that he wanted to be with me and only me. The jealousy I'd let take over for a minute almost felt silly.

"What's in the basket?" he asked as he tipped it toward him, a smile playing on his face.

"Oh, I wanted to bring you lunch. I know you're probably busy."

"Never too busy for you. Let's eat."

We took our time, talking about Paris and all the things we'd see and do there. I, of course, wanted the Eiffel tower to be the first stop. I knew it was cheesy, but I didn't care as long as I got to do it with Christian. We finished eating and kissed until my lips were numb. We only stopped because I had to pick up Annie.

"Should we tell her tonight?" I asked. "She's a smart kid. I mean I know she's going to figure it out eventually."

He nodded his emerald eyes twinkling at me. "I was just

thinking the same thing. Sure, let's take her out and tell her tonight. I'm sure she'll be thrilled, so don't look so nervous."

I scoffed. "Easy for you to say, she has to love you."

Christian yanked me against his chest. "And she already loves you. The same way I do."

My hands gripped his arms and I forgot how to speak.

He loves me?

I felt my heart fluttering like a trapped bird my chest and I kissed him once more, long and hard until I felt quite dizzy. I knew that if I didn't leave right that minute, we'd be naked and on his nice, expensive looking leather sofa in no time. And I wasn't the quietest person in the world, so yeah... that would be a very bad idea.

We said our goodbyes at the door a few too many times before I finally walked away. My mood was even better than it had been when I first arrived. I couldn't stop grinning. I could feel my cheeks starting to hurt, but I still didn't care. My future was finally coming together. That was the only thing that mattered.

I packed everything away into the car and pulled out. I couldn’t wait to call Natalie and rub it in her face. Lovingly, of course. I grinned because I knew she would totally see me as bragging but she'd laugh about it the whole time and be happy for me. She was one of the only people in my life that was over the moon about all the great things that ever happened to me. I knew I'd have to drag her out for coffee and tell her everything.

As I slowed to approach the upcoming red light, I realized that I wasn't really slowing down at all. I pushed my foot against the pedal, but nothing happened. Panic started to flood me as I pressed even harder until it was flush against the floor, but I was still going way too fast.

"Oh, my God. Betsy, don’t do this to me,” I yelled at the car. “Stop, stop, stop!"

No matter how much I demanded this didn't mean it was going to work. I plowed through the red light and turned in time to see a car hurtling toward me, its horn blasting. I could see the horrified expression on the driver’s white face. Time slowed down and everything started happing in slow motion.

There was a terrible crunching sound of metal hitting metal. I was jerked forward. Betsy had not air bag. Pain shot through my body even as my head hit something hard and darkness swallowed me whole.

Chapter Thirty-Four

CHRISTIAN

"Daddy, is Hannah going to die?" Annie's voice was filled with fear.

I pulled her towards me and hugged her small worried body against mine. "No, honey. Of course not." I pulled away so I could look into her eyes. "She'll be just fine. I promise."

She pushed her lower lip out. It was trembling. The sight broke my heart. "Then why can't I see her?"

"That's because she's just been operated on and she's sleeping."

"Can't we wake her up?"

"No, we'll have to wait for her to wake up on her own. You don't like being woken up while you are deep in sleep, do you?"

"No, but I wouldn't be angry if Hannah woke me up."

"I know darling, but she needs her sleep so she can get better quicker."

"Daddy will she be better by dinner."

"No honey. You're going to spend tonight with grandpa and grandma and I'm going to stay with Hannah and make sure she gets all the help she needs, okay?"

"Why I can't I stay too. I can help too."

"I'm sure Hannah would love that, but they don't allow children, honey." I glanced at my watch, then out of the square hospital windows. It was going to rain soon and I wished my parents would hurry up and come and pick Annie up. Especially since I wanted to go back to Hannah's bedside. Being away from her even for these few short minutes was making me feel edgy and nervous. I needed to there for her. I wanted her wake up and for me to see with my own eyes that she was fine. That everything was all right again.

"Daddy, if you want to marry Hannah, you can, you know?"

My head jerked around. "What?"

"I said, you can marry Hannah if you want. I won't mind."

I stared at her sweet face. It was impossible that she suspected Hannah and I were in love. We only just admitted it to ourselves. I made my voice gentle. "Why did you say that, honey?"

She gave a little shrug. "Mommy told me that all the nannies just want to marry you, and once they marry you, they will become like the evil stepmother in Cinderella."

I stared at her incredulously. Fuck you, and your ugly heart, Daphne. "Your mother told you that?"

She nodded. “But I don’t think Hannah is going to be evil to me, do you Daddy?”

I shook my head automatically. I was in too much shock to even get my head around the horrendous idea that my ex-wife had imprinted into her innocent daughter’s head. No wonder Annie had been so horrible to all her nannies. It all made sense now.

“I don’t think so either,” she agreed solemnly.

I took both Annie’s hands in mine. “Listen to me, Annie. Your mother was wrong to tell you that. That’s not how things happen. Most nannies don’t want to marry their employers. It’s just their job to take care of children so that the kids’ parents can work. Yes, some nannies do fall in love with some of their employers, but they don’t automatically turn into evil stepmothers. Do you understand that?”

“Why did Mommy say that then?”

“Maybe she was afraid you would stop loving her.”

She looked down at her shoes. “I don’t love her that much, Daddy.”

“It’s okay, honey. You just love who you want to love, okay?”

She looked up at me. “Okay.”

I grinned at her. “That’s my girl.”

“Daddy, do you think Hannah will fall in love with you?”

I swallowed. “Would you like that?”

“Yes, I want her to stay with us forever and ever...and ever.”

It was as if all my wishes had come true. “Let me see what I can do about that, okay?”

She grinned. “I can be the flower girl.”

I laughed. Things will work out, I could feel it in my bones.

Chapter Thirty-Five

HANNAH

Light flooded my eyes and I tried to blink it away.

My body felt so heavy and all I wanted to do was to go back to the soft darkness I had come from. Everything hurt. I groaned as I half-opened my eyes.

Christian peered at me closely. His eyes were rimmed with red, there were dark circles underneath them, and his clothes looked disheveled and messy. "Oh, thank God you're awake," he said with relief, as he stood and took my hand in his. "Can you hear me, Hannah?"

I nodded a little and winced at the pain. "What happened? I remember being in the car and I couldn't stop..." I trailed off.

Christian glared. There was a ring of white around his mouth. "Daphne is what happened. She hired someone to cut your brake fluid line. I'm so fucking pissed I let you leave on your own. I'm so sorry, Hannah. I would take your pain if I could."

"Shhh," I told him softly. "It's not your fault. You couldn't have known."

“I should have known,” he grated out in an anguished voice.

He looked so upset it broke my heart. “Don’t,” I whispered. “I’m alive and that all that counts.”

You’re alive by the grace of God,” he said bitterly.

“How bad is it?" I asked, trying my move my shoulder and feel pain ratcheting through my body. "Everything is killing me."

"You have a mild concussion from hitting your head on the steering wheel, you broke your arm, and the rest are bruises."

I glanced at my arm. "That would explain the cast.” I closed my eyes. “Ugh...and the pain."

Christian touched my cheek gently. It felt like a butterfly wing brushing against my skin.

I opened my eyes. He looked as if he was afraid even to touch me properly because he felt I might break. Honestly, I could understand why. I felt like I would break too. My eyes filled with tears and I watched with surprise as his did the same.

"It's okay. Everything's going to be fine," he said as he laid his head on mine so tenderly that I could barely feel it.

"What if she does this again?" I whispered. "She really hates me, Christian."

"I told you I'll protect you. She's already sitting in jail waiting to hear her fate. Gabriel refused to bail her out because of who he is, and she can't access any of the funds that were in their account. She has no choice but to answer for what she's done and so does he. Thank God, the security cameras at my building caught her and the man she hired together, as she pointed out your car. My security detail called the police immediately after they saw him go over and get under your car. I'm going to make sure she stays in prison for a long, long time."

Relief flooded me. Now that I knew there was no chance she could come back to haunt us, I could breathe freely again. Christian kissed me gently and I kissed him back, just happy to be alive and with him.

"God, I love you so much, Hannah," he whispered desperately against my cheek.

"I love you too," I whispered before I let the drugs take me back into soft, painless blackness.

Chapter Thirty-Six

HANNAH

I hated not being able to do anything, but Christian had put me on strict bedrest orders. Not only that, he'd hired a new nanny, a lovely girl that was upbeat and chipper with Annie. Annie had given her a hard time for all of five minutes until I asked her to be nice and give it a chance. In the end, she was a good nanny and Annie started to like her. If I thought I was super Nanny, Patricia was that times ten. I had no idea how she had so much energy.

Weeks went by and I finally got my cast off.

I'd been so happy my arm was healed and I could finally take our Paris trip. We'd dropped Annie off with Christian's parents early in the morning and got on his private jet.

"I can't believe you have one of these." I sighed as I walked around. "It's so cool."

"I'll buy one for you too," he said as he pulled me into his arms.

"Don't be dramatic. I'm just admiring it, that's all."

Christian chuckled. "You know I can't help it. The minute you say you like something, I want to buy ten of them for you."

I touched his cheek. "That's because you're the sweetest man who has ever walked this earth. I am so glad that none of the women you were with realized it before me. Thank God, for dumb females."

He grinned, then led me back to the bedroom.

I still couldn't believe my eyes. It was lavishly done in gold and white. Hell, it was at least a hundred times better than my old bedroom at my apartment. Christian tugged me onto the bed and I knew I'd be occupying it for the next few hours doing my favorite thing with my favorite person.

We spent a long while getting great use of the Jet bed, then slept, then went at it again, until it was time to land and I had renewed energy all over again. My feet couldn't wait to touch Paris soil. I already had a list of restaurants I wanted to try and museums I wanted to visit.

"You're going to drag me all over, aren't you?" Christian asked as he watched how excited I was.

"Of course! Isn't that what girlfriends do?" I asked.

"You're not wrong about that, but I can't say that I mind at all." His green eyes sparkled at me.

The minute we were off the jet and into the bustling city, I was in awe. Everything was so new and different. I only knew minimal French having brushed up on my high school skills while I was laid up in bed. Christian, however, was damn near fluent. The minute he said anything in French, I was ready to jump him all over again. On his yummy lips, it just sounded so sexy.

"Where should we go first?" he asked.

I think I ended up being led around as much as he did. Christian ate where I wanted to eat and took me to all the touristy destinations, but he also dragged me to expensive, upscale boutiques for clothes, jewelry, and shoes.

I looked at one price tag and almost fainted. "I really don't need anything," I tried to insist.

"Nonsense. You like it, right?"

I pursed my lip and ran a finger down the silken spine of a gorgeous emerald dress I admired. "It's pretty, but I wouldn't pay that price."

"I would," he said.

I smiled instead of objecting. I knew how much it meant to Christian to spoil me and I didn't mind being spoiled in such a dreamy city. It was a special occasion, I wouldn't even fuss about it because as Natalie said, *'You went for it and now, you deserve it. Go for it girl!'*

"When are we going to see the Eiffel tower?" I asked.

"When it's nice and dark," he replied and picked out a few more things. "It looks nice lit up at night."

I smiled. "You're a sap when you want to be."

"That's for sure," he said pulling his black American Express out.

That evening, I wore the emerald dress that he'd liked so much on me. He looked at me as if he couldn't believe his eyes. Anyone would think I was an angel come down from heaven. I rolled my eyes.

Dinner was lavish and expensive, and the food was to die for. It was so good that by the time we were done, I was ready to curl up with a bottle of champagne, make love to him, and pass out in his arms.

"One more stop, remember?" he reminded me.

I sat up straighter as I felt excited all over again. "That's right, the Eiffel tower. I can't wait to see it."

Christian squeezed my hand and led me out of the car.

When we arrived, I gasped. He was right. I'd seen it online, but nothing compared to the grandeur and beauty of it lit up like this... up close. My heart swelled with appreciation and I dabbed at my eyes. "I know I'm being cheesy and commercial, but this is so beautiful," I whispered.

"Not nearly as beautiful as you."

I glanced down at him in surprise when I saw he had shifted down to one knee. In his hand, he had a blue velvet box. My mouth opened. He had brought me to the Eiffel tower to propose? It must be a dream. Or some romance movie I made up in my head.

He opened it and showed off a ring that was so beautiful I stared between it and him. I'd suddenly lost any skill to speak or think coherently.

He stared up at me his green orbs shining. " You make me the happiest man alive. Every day when I wake up, I realize it's because of you that I've turned back into who I was meant to be. Remember how cranky I was in the beginning?"

I laughed and nodded as tears slipped down my face. "So cranky it used to drive me nuts and make me want to pick on you."

He grinned. "Well, you changed that. I want to make you happy for the rest of my life. Will you marry me, Hannah Gray?"

Now, here was something I didn't even have to think about. I nodded vigorously as tears splashed down my cheeks. I couldn't speak as I threw my arms around him. When I pulled back, he slipped the ring onto my finger.

People were clapping and cheering around us.

I never cried so hard in my life.

"I love you too much," he whispered as his lips brushed against mine.

"And I love you from the bottom of my heart," I whispered back.

Christian kissed me and my knees went weak.

At that moment, the only thing that existed was us. I can tell you now, I was damn happy to become the future Mrs. West.

Damn happy.

The End

ABOUT THE AUTHOR

Thank you so much for reading!

Do come visit me here:

ALSO BY RIVER

Cinderella.com

Taken By The Baller

Daddy's Girl

Dear Neighbor

The CEO and I

Kissing Booth

The Promise

Dare Me

Single Dad

Accidental Rivals

Too Hot To Handle

Sweet Revenge

CherryPopper

The Magic Cupcake

Never Catch the Bouquet

Pretend For Me

Let's Pretend

Pretend You're Mine

Printed by Amazon Italia Logistica S.r.l.
Torrazza Piemonte (TO), Italy

11655423R00123